Reviews

Michael Kiser's book, "The End Times" is an example of a "think piece", because it does do that very thing. As he attempts to explain that we have been "programmed" to believe a certain way by the religions of the world, while attempting to prove that other beings in conjunction with religious leaders on Earth have conspired from the beginning to not only alter the DNA of species in order to produce humans on this world through thousands of years of manipulations – and failures – but to make the reader think in a different way than he has before. Michael continues to explain the different species that came before mankind. He also points to the religious leaders, as well as governments, who have withheld the truth from man for eons. It is they who have controlled us from the outset over what we can do, think, and even believe while hiding the full truth of enlightenment from the rest of mankind.

LK Kelley – Author of The White Wolf Prophecy Trilogy & Book Editor

~~~
~~~

Reviews

Authors List of Books

Battling Guillain Barre Syndrome / Acute Relapsing
CIDP

~~~^~~

The End Times – What Is It Really About?

~~^~~

4 Book Series
"A Journey Into The Spiritual Quest Of Who We Are"
Book 1
~ The Reawakening –
Book 2
~ Why Were They Called gods –
Book 3
~The Knowledge That Was Once Forbidden By Some Of
The Ancient Beings –
Book 4
~ The Quantum Leap Into Consciousness –
~~~

The End Times –
What Is It Really About?

By
Michael J. Kiser

Edited by
L K Kelley

DragonEye Publishing

The End Times – What Is It Really About?

Cover Design By Michael J. Kiser
Editor: L K Kelley

ISBN 13: 978-0-9767832-9-9 Trade Paperback
ISBN 13: 978-1-61500-074-6 (Ebook)

Library of Congress Catalog Number: 2009936982

Published by Ancient Civilizations, an Imprint of DragonEye Publishing

www.DragonEyePublishers.com
Orders@DragonEyePublishers.com

DragonEye Publishing
753A Linden Place
Elmira, NY 14901 USA

DragonEye Publishing First Edition: December 2009
First Printing: December 2009
Second Printing January 2017

10 9 8 7 6 5 4 3 2

Manufactured in the United States of America

Contents

Page

Preface

Over the past 35 years I have spent delving deep into all these World religions, along with talking to hundreds of people that lives their life based on their religion. These people have looked at my previous 4 Book series called, 'A Journey Into The Spiritual Quest Of Who We Are', which they have mentioned that they did not want to read any books that deals with Metaphysical or Spirituality.

Therefore, what I am doing with this book is to bring a book about life base of these religious beliefs that is spread across all corners of our World, and there are thousands of books on this. Nevertheless, I plan to show how all these religions are all connected regardless of what region or what part of the world you live in.

You might have a question, is this even possible? The answer is yes, it can be. It is through all of the religions that want you to think that they are 'The Chosen One' by this one being, that is called (GOD), and that all other people are not the chosen one.

Now for those people that have my other books called, 'A Journey Into The Spiritual Quest Of Who We Are', have mentioned that the books are short, but they are packed with straight to the point with vital knowledge that answers the many questions that we all have in our life.

In addition, this book 'The End Times – What Is It Really About?' also has no exceptions to any one religion, as you will see.

This book is not for any one religion, but it is for all religions…

As you Journey through this Book, you will also learn 'The Truth' of what has not been taught to you through any and of all of the religions that exists around our world called Earth.

The reason behind that is that no world religions want you to know the truth that is being hold from all. I have been involved in delving into all of the world religions since 1979 to unlock the truth that is being hidden from all of us, in order to keep all of us from evolving to who we really are.

Chapter 1

The Young Leading the Old

For the past 12,000 years, these early generations were raised to believe and to fear all changes that the Earth was experiencing. 'Lightning, Floods, Earthquakes, Volcanoes, and Famines are only a few upheavals that were transpiring, resulting in the people believing that these events were due to the wrath of their 'God', or the 'Devil'.

As time progressed, bards who were known as "story tellers", used poems in either recitation or singing to recite stories about these events to others as they traveled around their country, as well as bordering countries, across the oceans, and eventually, when writing was established, through the written word. Even today, after thousands of generations have passed, the many belief systems still re-tell the same stories within the vast majority of every country and culture. Thus, we have all been raised from the time we are young to believe these same stories whether or not they come through religion. Until another culture arrived in their own civilization, those who had no contact with the outside world thought that these stories were theirs alone until another culture arrived.

Fear drives much of our belief systems. Churches, Temples, of any other religions have driven the fear within us against beings of "Good" and "Evil" as they bring their battles to planet Earth fighting for dominion. These images of battles of good and evil are burned into our minds through these ancient stories are true, and the "proof" of it is written within "The Bible", and other ancient manuscripts. If we do not do as we are told by the word of "God", or "gods", punishment will be swift. A Supreme Being exists within most all religious books, such as "The Bible". This being is known by many names, such as 'GOD - Jesus' in Christianity, 'Jehovah, Yahovah, Yahweh, Ohrmazda, Mohammed, along with hundreds of other names.

As I mentioned in my four book series, 'A Journey Into The Spiritual Quest Of Who We Are', I applied example after example for how, and why these beings designed and created this fear.

The Beings who evolved prior to humans created veils of illusions. They jealously and selfishly guarded their knowledge of life while deliberately preventing humans from evolving and joining their ranks, because humans were beneath them. They did not want other life forms butting into their knowledge, which they considered theirs - alone. Armed with the truth of this knowledge of life, they created a way to hide the truth from humans, effectively preventing them from learning what, and who, they could become. Therefore, they not only posed as older humans, they created lies in the guise of stories. Thus, the younger, human generations were misdirected by continual repetition of the lies. Through repetition, these beings realized that if lies are repeated often enough, eventually, humans would no longer ask questions about whom, or where, their place was in life. They also realized that they needed to do so through the *young humans*, because older humans are not as acceptable to change. Once these lies were created and continually repeated, they became embedded into the minds of young humans. From generation to generation - each embellishing the lies as time progressed, these beliefs morphed into "gods". Certain humans realized that the power associated with these "gods", could be tremendous, and they could control their tribes, towns, cities, and even nations in any way they wished. The few who understood this, began to develop the first religions based upon the lies, and a hierarchy was established within religion, which gave these humans great power over how all other humans believed.

Finally, the influence of the lies became real, and no human ever questioned the truth, again. More and more religious beliefs were established and divided. This gave the higher beings full, and total control over humans and civilizations. Therefore, by these beliefs, it became easy to manipulate the human world. Their misdirection worked! It is not surprising that there is no doubt that we all still live in fear of these beings. The ancient beings were firmly ensconced into our world as "gods", a specific theme entwined around them. At first, humans believed their "gods" had nothing but respect and love for humans. In time, a new idea arose. Humans began to believe that the "gods" *manipulated* human history, and cared nothing for the human world. The idea that they sat upon their thrones, and played with human lives, became well known throughout the world, and this belief flourished as it spread. "Gods" were simply acting roles, and calling themselves "gods". Human belief in them dwindled. While these ancient "gods" were pushed aside long ago, some of the most popular remain in our religions, today.

Within my other books, it is obvious that for the last 2,000 - 3,000 years to the present, no one has seen the so-called "gods" in which our ancestors believed. However, it is truly amazing that even today, people *still* fear the same stories in books such as, ‘The Bible’, as well as other books and/or scrolls.

It is quite obvious that earthquakes, weather/climate, volcanoes, floods, and other earth changing events are no more than normal for our Earth. Even in the event of illnesses and plagues, today’s humans no longer believe there is no “god” or “devil” causing these events. They are all *natural* events, and many of them are cyclical. In the face of the age of the Earth, and the fact that documentation of “normal” was not available until the mid-1800’s, perhaps it is time to blame ourselves for some of the Earth changes that mankind has created.

Humankind devised the ideas of religion with “gods”, “devils”, as well as other deities, were made simply because they did not want to take the blame for some of the things erupting around humankind. Instead of judging ourselves, the need to have a great being judge us seems to be inborn into us. Why humans have not caught on by now is puzzling.

After hearing the same, repetitive stories without witnessing a single “god” worldwide, people still say, “god says I must believe and act this way - or else.”

Some people, when asked if they have seen a “god”, say, “No. There is no one next to me. But, I heard a voice, which told me that I must believe this way.”

But, truth be known, if I heard a voice, I would ask him to prove he is a "god". Knowing that all beings evolve at different times in existence, this still does not make saying one is a "god" is true! The stories are nothing more than what they are - stories. Because of the wide belief in the existence of a "god" and/or "devil", humans will still not question them, but instead, they pass them down to the subsequent generations. As long as this fear is within each of us, we will never ask questions. And, if they do, others will point and call them stupid or ignorant. And, because of others' beliefs in religion, the perpetuation will continue to grow. Another problem that mankind seems to possess is that most all of us live in fear of *asking* questions! In school, who voluntarily raises their hand to ask a question when surrounded by their peers and friends? Answer is…most all of us!

By creating confusion, it would be easy to keep humans in a "stagnant evolution". By continuing to perpetuate the idea that "gods" will judge you based only upon religious beliefs while embellishing these stories as time progresses, it continues to confuse humans. In fact, because the stories do change is the very reason that they are kept alive as they are passed down to man. Designed this way keeps the confusion and fear flowing from age to age.

What a terrible way to live life! To be

controlled by other beings who pretend to be “gods”! Why would anyone consider living a life under this condition? One is nothing more than a puppet and the strings are being pulled from thousands of years ago! Why would one surrender the essence or energy of life to others who seek to control not only you, but also those who come after you!

Throughout my four book series, ‘A Journey Into The Spiritual Quest Of Who We Are’, I have attempted to explain that they use different ways to control us. Humiliating us into believing what they tell us is the main way to keep us from asking questions. Therefore, we continue in ignorance, and our puppeteers pull at our strings.

These veils are subtle, and are used in stories, books, television, movies, and now, the internet. The following are two examples.

Example #1 is based on the Star Wars movies with the use of The Force, which can create both positive and negative energies. One is a being drawn to negative energy. It is used to control others, because the perception is that their power is stronger. Humans are forced to bow down to these beings while continuing to live in fear of being destroyed. This keeps them in constant fear, and so, they obey. This is an example of negative energy.

Example #2 is from the movie Stargate, the

TV series, Stargate SG-1, into Stargate: Atlantis. A being known as the "Goa'uld" (pronounced "go-a-uld"). These beings evolved as far as possible in their real form. Yet, can no longer continue to live without a host to survive. Thus, it is, essentially, a parasite. However, by taking a host, usually human, it can give the human a few extra hundred years until that body becomes unsustainable, and the parasite must leave that body to seek another. The human is pushed to the side, but with the Goa'uld taking over the mind of the human. It is feasible that this serpent being could live indefinitely as long as there are unlimited humans to serve as hosts. In this case, they make sure humans continue to breed by masquerading as "gods". The Goa'uld conquers civilizations, and by using some magical "mumbo-jumbo" that the humans have never seen, evoke fear within the population by severe punishment, which stops the humans from trying to seek a way to freedom. Therefore, with humans, the Goa'uld have a continuing supply of hosts.

This is a perfect example of what I am attempting to prove. By keeping humans ignorant of the truth, their beliefs are set, and no one questions the truth. In this case, humans from Earth believe in another type of deity, and not in the Goa'uld. Once this group begins to question who these beings are, they quickly discover the lie of the “gods” in the past on Earth.

It is all about control. Period. The stories create the illusion of “gods” followed by repetition to the young that perpetuates fear among the population. The stories continue to be passed on, and humans are gullible. They will believe anything that gives them a glimpse of hope.

Except for some, most of everyone today has lived their life by these stories. In addition, it is their strong, religious belief that keeps humans in fear of being punished. We are conditioned not to ask by religious doctrines.

But, there are those of us who are not fooled by the truth. Control is no longer binding them to a spark – a light within them that awakened us, and realize that everything around them are nothing but illusions, which are controlling them. Then, humans begin their journey of a spiritual quest in order to learn who a human is.

Heads of the major religions, especially, are not taking this lightly. They know that they will lose their control and, more importantly, their power over the people. As this expands, the loss of this power angers them. As more people begin to shed these veils, they begin to see the truth about life.

When all else has failed, now, they lay claim the End Times are here. For over 12,000 years, humans have heard this. Yet, still, more and more people are leaving churches, synagogues, temples, and other religions despite the constant testimony about the End Times, and Earth changes such as droughts, plagues, earthquakes, floods, and volcanoes are proof of this. And, we are told that every 1000 years, a battle of good and evil comes on Earth. All to see which group will be victorious enough to rule humans for another 1000 years. And, finally, a massive war will descend onto Earth to end our existence in this life. In this case, this is the current belief.

Materialism vs. Spiritualism

Life is truly complex. Some people say life is nothing more than being born. They believe it is only living to a certain age, and then, you. Your soul is sent "somewhere" where a "God", or "gods", judges your works, and that decision places you for all of eternity. This could be "heaven" or "hell", "purgatory", "Hades", or the "Elysian Fields". It depends upon the belief and doctrine of the religion one in which one is a member.

But, there is more to life than being born, dying, or being judged. Mankind breeze through life with millions upon millions of experiences - from the smallest which we do not always notice to the life altering experiences. Death is just one of many life-altering experiences, and is the very one we refuse to acknowledge until someone close to us dies. Then, we are forced to confront it. We ask many questions:

"Why did this person have to die?"

"Why did this person have to die in this manner?"

And, of course, the most important one word question that encompasses all of it, yet taught not to ask?

Simply - "Why?"

No answer comes, and understanding eludes us.

Six billion people on Earth, and each one of us has different and unique experiences. It is quite surprising that no two of us have the same experience. In order to understand where we fit into the world, and why we have different experiences, we must understand the complexity and the consciousness of our world, before we can begin to understand our place on Earth, and then, to look within our own existence and experiences.

Despite growing up in different cultures and/or beliefs, most realize that Earth is a living entity that has lived through eons of time. It is ageless. And, if it could talk, imagine what it could tell us! Some truly believe, as do I, that the Earth has its own consciousness - that it is a highly evolved being. That it is alive. But, perhaps the Earth is speaking to us? Proof exists in the weather, volcanoes, earthquakes, collisions with celestial bodies, floods, and so much more. No day is the same around the world. Just the thought of it is too immense and spans time itself.

But, why is this happening? The Earth tilts upon its axis and flips randomly throughout its existence. Sometimes, slowly while other times instantly. Even though it has not happened in man's memory does not mean it does not happen. Humanity is a bit too arrogant to believe that they know the Earth's past, when the opposite is true. These events causes oceans to shift to new locations moving over the continents changing main lands and islands alike. And, as the oceans flood over the landscape, the waters destroy civilized cities in different time periods - essentially wiping them from existence while forcing those lucky enough to have survived to higher ground, or ships. The lost knowledge with that destruction becomes new, yet again, as mankind relearns all of it through years, and it could very well take thousands of years to relearn what was lost. What they believe is new land far away is nothing more than the changing landscape. Continents, which were, are no more. Islands, which were, are no more. Both being replaced by the receding floods while reshaping the dry land. The world they knew is, now, gone.

Thus, civilizations begin anew.

In addition to the changes in, and on, the Earth, man's soul and/or spirit also changes. The International Society for Krishna Consciousness is one of the many movements for the spiritual reorientation of man through a simple process of chanting the holy names of god. It is believed that humans should realize that our material life ends in nothing less than misery. While everyone else bustles about in their material ways, this Society is trying to end these miseries. Yet, it points out that even with the procurement of material existence, it is only a temporary happiness for man. Unfortunately, many scientists deny the existence of anything spiritual, and that it is, ultimately, the living force within each human. Science cannot explain all, nor can they explain why as man's physical body changes, so does the mind, spirit, and soul.

Earth undergoes changes of night and as well as four seasons in many places. Others see only one or two seasons. The more primitive mentalities attributed this phenomenon to our star that is called 'Apsu', or the Sun. Primitive people thought the sun was getting weaker, and presumed at night that the sun was dead when it was simply rising in another part of the world. Today, we are far more advanced, and we see that the sun does not change at all, but the changes are due simply by the relative positions of the Earth to the Sun. Just as primitive tribes believe that the sun dies at sunset, those with less intelligence, but who believe they are more intelligent, presume that after death, the spirit's existence is forever finished. However, unknown to modern society, once the body becomes old, the soul sheds it like an old garment and accepts another body.

The "constitutional position" of the soul is due strictly to manmade belief systems, which keep man from the truth. Departments in different universities, and / or many technological institutions, study the subtle laws of a material nature. There are also medical research laboratories, which study the physiological condition of the material body, but there is no institution to study the "constitutional position" of the soul. This is the greatest drawback of materialistic civilization, which is simply an external manifestation of the soul.

While people are enamored of the human body, or even the cosmic bodies, they do not understand the true basic principle. While all of it is beautiful, man attributes energy and traits to talent and brains, but the moment the soul leaves the body, the body becomes useless. Scientists cannot trace personal self. Yet, it is the soul that is the cause of the incredible discoveries that science has made.

~ The Krsna Consciousness Movement

through science and philosophy is trying to make others aware of the soul. While not through dogma, they seek to do so through scientific and philosophical understanding to which one can perceive the presence of a super soul and consciousness, which resides in man's mortal consciousness.

~ In the Vedanta sutra, or the Vedanta philosophy, absolute truth is explained through the Srimad – Bhagavatam, which is a commentary by the same author, and the Bhagavatam – gita is the preliminary study of the Srimad - Bhagavatam for understanding the constitutional position of the supreme lord, or the absolute truth. ~

The Three Aspects of the Soul

Consciousness and heart, or the spirit and person. The absolute truth consists in the impersonal Brahman, followed by "one's own point of view of GOD". It becomes a localized super soul (Paramatma), and as the supreme personality of a godhead representing "all" - Krsna. Krsna exists simultaneously with Brahman, Paramatma, and Godhead. Moreover, it is similar to mankind in both soul and person - two consciousness's.

The individual person and the supreme person exist as one, but are also different and separate. For example,... a drop of seawater is as individual as every other drop, but each drop is also a collective part of the whole sea, yet their chemical compositions are the same. With the addition of salt and other minerals, their content within the sea is much greater than that within a drop of seawater. Like the seawater example, the Krsna Movement upholds both the individuality of the soul and the supreme soul. From the Vedic Upanishads, the supreme person, or god, and the individual person are eternal and living entities. Other faith-based beliefs want us to believe that the drop of seawater and the sea are separate, and that the Supreme Being controls us. In Christianity, the Bible teaches the same principle is said that forgiveness is only available through prayer to the Supreme Father for their individual sins as well as the whole. Man must have a constant in their lives, and this serves our consciousness well. Otherwise, without it, there will be chaos, which is created by religions to keep control over man, so that we do not realize that the true meaning is that mankind is really part of a collective - the "God".

As we enter the New Age, understanding of this knowledge is gradually reawakening.

As absolute power escalates, everyone wants to become the Supreme Lord in all walks of life: socially, politically, individually, and collectively. This is someone, according to the Krsna Conscience Movement, who has attained a human body and intelligence in order to understand, because this consciousness makes his life successful.

Religions do not want the individual to realize any of this, because when individual humans learn that all combined is this “god”, then they lose their control over us. Those who control religions will go to any extent to hold power over us. However, it does not end with religion. On the contrary, world governments also control their people with fear through wars. Almost five thousand years ago, a war on the battlefields of Kuruksetra, confirms this.

Krsna offered this consciousness to the Bhagavad – Gita. It was also given to the sun god, Vivasvan, at least 120,000,000 years ago. While this movement is as old as time itself, it was handed down to all the great leaders of India’s Vedic civilization, including Sankaracarya, Ramanujacarya, Madhvacarya,Vishnu Svami, Nimbarka, ‘IESU – Immanuel – Jesus’, and finally, about 600 years ago, Lord Cartanya. This discipline is even followed today, and used widely in all parts of the world by great scholars, philosophers, and religionists. However, in most cases, the principles are not being followed correctly. The Krsna Consciousness Movement presents the principles of the Bhagavad – Gita as they are – without any misinterpretation.

There are five main principles in the Bhagavad – Gita.

1) a god
2) a living entity
3) nature (material and spiritual)
4) time
5) activities (not eternal)

All are eternal except for the fifth - activities which are of a material nature, and quite different from activities in the spiritual nature. Through the spirit, the soul is eternal, and the activities performed under the influence of the material nature are temporary. The Krsna Consciousness Movement aims at placing the spirit within eternal activities. Practicing these eternal activities, even when we are materially engaged to act spiritually, simply requires direction. Difficult, yes, but possible under prescribed rules and regulations.

Continue to remember…religions are keeping man stagnant. They do not wish us to know the *truth* about Who We Are. These religions place rules and regulations in place, which keep humans from going beyond a certain point, and to never look beyond that point.

The Krsna Consciousness Movement

teaches these spiritual activities. If one is trained in these, one is transferred to the spiritual world by a change of consciousness. It here where evidence from the Vedic literatures, including the Bhagavad – Gita, is shown. One does not need to be trained, to enter this spiritual world. The spiritual world is all around us. It is within us. Look within yourself, and anyone will be able to see that spiritual world by meditation. Even dreams are other realms, which we cannot see through our physical eyes.

All Consciousness's are always present. They interact with all of us, and we are interacting with the soul spirit. Perception of those other realms, however, is consistently contaminated with false knowledge. For instance, rain is pure and clear. However, as soon as the water comes in touch with the ground, it becomes muddy, and it is difficult to see through it. Yet, if we filter the same water, the original clarity returns. Clearing our consciousness allows one to gain eternal life of knowledge and bliss. Material life keeps us ignorant, and while the leaders of human society should take this reawakening of the consciousness movement very seriously, it is being ignored.

Believing there is a one god in control of everything is changing. In addition, as we make this transition into the New Age on December 21, 2012, many religious appear to realize it. As we

Journey into the unknown, man will learn the knowledge of life. Mankind will reawaken to this knowledge of consciousness, essence, and connection to the energy life force, which binds all life together. Through this reawakening of our consciousness, man will realize that he creates his *own existence*. Man's near future is being created through an energy force, which is not far beyond our reach.

This unknown knowledge is what we will use as we create our future from our past.

Chapter 2

The Beginnings of Human Civilization

When did human civilization start? We are just beginning to realize that human civilization has been on Earth for innumerable thousands of years. Most all religions have concluded that human civilization only had one beginning, and that was approximately eight thousand years ago in 6000 BCE (Before Current Era). While each religion claims that their civilization was first, they all have the same story of the end of those civilizations - corruption of man by the devil, or Fallen Angels.

With each story, even though there are slight differences, the basic story is the same; even though reference to time for creation is never mentioned other than the Universe was created in six days.

Stages of Creation are as follows:

1. Chaos existed without form
2. "God" (by whatever name is used), created the universe
3. Creation of Earth
4. Creation of Animals
5. Creation of man
6. Creation of woman from the rib of man (Adam and Eve)
7. "God" rests on the seventh Day

For one to understand the meaning of the creation of humans, a need to understand how life was created on Earth, or any other world existing within the Universe.

In order to understand this we must, now…

…Re-Learn The Origin of Life

"God", or "gods", we are told, created the universe, the stars, (The Heavens), the planets, and life on Earth. When asked if others believe that intelligent life exists on other planets, sixty percent say -"No, I don't. There is no other intelligent life within the Universe other than human beings." Forty percent of the people will say, "If there is no other intelligent life in the universe, then why would someone expend energy creating the Universe just for us?. Why not just make the solar system only?"

The stories also state that we are made in "God's" image. Then, why are all the different races and colors present? Perhaps it does not mean his image as to these things. Perhaps it means his physical form of one who stand upright on two legs. Who has two arms, a body, and a head. Maybe he injects colors and races into his general "image". Image simply means "a likeness" to another. Then, the general appearance of a human *is* in his image. So, the idea of our being in "God's image", or "God's likeness" is true for nowhere does it say we are made in his image with race and/or color.

If each religion claims that "God" created their religion, does it not follow that all religions are of "God", regardless? And, would it also not follow that he created animals in his image as well? And, if this is so, it would further follow that other life could exist anywhere within his Universe.

And, "God" also gave us choice. There are two paths to follow: darkness and light; good and evil. Freewill is what distinguishes us from other life forms.

Earth took billions of millions of years to

create. The proof is in Science, and not religious beliefs which say that Earth is only 4,000 years old. Some religions have added 2000 years, now, making it 6000, or even 9000 years old. Even as in science where the presence of man is being pushed backward into time in great leaps, it appears the same is happening within the religious communities. When religion and science discover the same thing, we must open our eyes to truth.

We all know that life was created by something, or from someone. While we all will continue to argue this point, none can deny that life started somewhere. However, some will never change their minds no matter what evidence is placed in front of their eyes.

Worlds began to shape after the Big Bang. Whether stars, planets, asteroids, comets, etc. Until grabbed by a sun, worlds were covered with ice several miles thick, and have no atmosphere or liquid water. Europa, a moon of Jupiter, is a the perfect example.

Once one of these bodies is drawn toward the gravity of a star, this ice begins to melt revealing oceans. From its beginnings, an awakening begins. DNA, vital to the formation of life is within the liquid now exists, and the living organisms, once lying embedded within that ice, become animate evolving throughout hundreds of years until they reach the Primordial complex organisms.

The planet begins another evolution process during the Primordial age when these complex organisms begin to change. 'The Life-Coders', beings of other worlds, begin to evolve from their infant forms into both non-physical and physical forms. At the same time, a group of beings, known as "Eunuch", arrives from a planet in nearby star system when a humanoid presence is detected. These beings are humanoid in feature. The Eunuch are of both genders - Male and Female. These beings bring forth the humanoid race to all planets suitable for human life to exist.

"Life-Coders", or gods, prepare to leave Earth when all life forms on this planet begin to experience a metamorphosis stage that merges the spirit with the physical body. The life forms that exists on this planet are mammals, reptiles, human, humanoid creatures such as apes, right along with the spirits. During this metamorphosis all beings of both physical and non-physical form enter into a stasis of deep sleep. During this stage, memories of their prior, physical life are forgotten, but is still recorded within the non-physical form, or what we call the spirit or soul.

Lost is the cognizant knowledge of the past and their arrival on Earth as the original beings awaken to a whole new existence.

For purposes of brevity, "Life-Coders" will be referred to as "gods". To help the new beings understand that they have both the physical, and non-physical within them, these "gods" physically interacted with the awakening beings of this planet. Throughout the metamorphosis which lasts about one hundred years, they are taught that they existed as two separate beings for about five thousand years prior. As time evolves, each civilization on Earth renews from time to time, and with it, the single, basic beginnings remain indelible over all of the generations and civilizations.

Stories of Adams and Eves of the past

What religions around the world do not wish you to know, I will impart to you about the true stories of humans. Each new beginning of the human life cycle is called the…

"Human Growth Evolution" or "Adam and Eve"

For those who delve into the stories of past civilizations on Earth, we have discovered that most date back to Adam and Eve. But, there are other, earlier, human stories existing before Adam and Eve - long before the civilizations that we do know. Far more than one story of the famous classic Bible story and the creation of human life.

All churches teach of the past, and most all of us know of one story told over and over again about Adam and Eve being the first of all humans on Earth keeping the truth of our past from us.

But, there are more stories of an earlier Adam and Eve. Two of these earlier stories, I have brought to light in two of my earlier books called, "The Bridge From A Distant World" part of my four book series called, "The Spiritual Journey Of Who We Are", and in book 2, "Why were They called Gods?".

Eunuchs

Between 200,000 and 24,000 years ago, a being who was both male and female, existed upon Earth - The Eunuch. Most left Earth about 2000 years ago into the stars around our galaxy, but some stayed for approximately 16,000 years. As Earth changes began increasing around 14,000 years ago BCE, the rest of them departed from the surface of Earth 12,000 years BCE.

On the continent of Tampaurban which was Africa, and now called the Middle East, two of the oldest of these ancient stories is known as

'The Eunuch's'.

The Eunuch (Eu-nu-K)

The "Eunuch" was beings of both sex genders existing upon the earth until the last completion of the cycle in which our group of stars exists. These same stars make their way around our galaxy. 12,000 years ago, the Eunuch had to depart, as I mentioned above, due to the energies that the earth was experiencing. One must be able to translate these stories in order to understand them.

On the continent of Tampaurban, ancient stories document these beings. Shortly after approximates 12,000 years, they began to change. They separated into individuals of male and female which is known as the pre-human race. They differ in that they had no belly button at all.

After the separation, they still lived for thousands of years. This story is the same one that most all other cultures have in their ancient histories - each being similar - including that of the Bible, and from this race came the human race of today.

200,000 Years Ago

Eons ago, on the edge of a unique galaxy known as ‘The Milky Way Galaxy’, fifteen worlds orbited a star called, “Apsu”. Out of these, there were four worlds, and one of those worlds was called “Ki” - Earth, or Terra.

Eunuch starships approached the world of “Ki”, landing upon one of its largest Continents, calling it “Tampaurban”. The Ruwenzori Mountains are surrounded by a dense forest. This is where the ships landed. Four waterfalls flood over all four sides of the mountain into a lush valley below, creating four rivers which divide the land into four sections complete with exotic trees and flowers. Here was where they lived, and there lived, also, “the most high of the creator of beings”.

Some of the Eunuch’s began to build pyramids and temples surrounded by cities, while others traveled to other continents to see what other types of beings occupied this lush world.

From continent to continent, they

discovered beings of humanoid - serpents, humanoid-reptilians, and humanoid - sectoids. But, they also discovered beings of the non-physical form, and that was all they did find. No humans existed. What they did learn was that these beings were from other planets within the Milky Way Galaxy, as well as from other realms.

Around 180,000 BCE, about ten percent of Eunuchs living on 'Ki - Earth', decided to leave this world for other habitable planets orbiting its star, "Apsu", while the non-physical beings stayed on Earth and in other realms existing around the Earth.

The First Story Ever Told

Early Eunuchs created humanoid-male and humanoid-female hybrids by altering the indigenous life forms on Earth through DNA patterns and methods of Cryogenics.

According to the Bible, God let Adam name every beast, bird, and other living things. When they passed before him in pairs, **Adam**, who was about twenty years-old, became jealous of the love each had. **Adam tried coupling with each female creature in turn**, but found no satisfaction in the act. He therefore cried:

"Every creature, but me has a proper mate!" So, he prayed to God that he would remedy this injustice. [Gen. 17.4; B. Yebamot

63a] God formed Lilith, the first woman, as he had done Adam, except with filth and sediment instead of pure dust. Unfortunately, they never found peace together. When he wished to lay with her, she took offence at the recumbent position.

"Why must I lie beneath you?" she asked. "I also was made from dust, and am therefore your equal."

From Adam's union with this **demoness,** and with another like her named **Naamah,** Tubal Cain's sister was born, and from her came **Asmodeus, a demon,** and innumerable **demons** that still plague mankind. Many generations later, these two women, **Lilith** and **Naamah,** came to Solomon disguised as harlots who were fighting over the birth of a baby - each of them claiming to be hers. [Yalqut Reubeni *ad. Gen. II.* 21; IV. 8]

After 10,000 years of creating these hybrids, they realized that their hybrids were not useful, so, they let these beings of humanoid-humans were allowed to leave to populate other parts of Tampaurban.

Thus, this first attempt at human creation failed, and…

…The Second Attempt at Human Creation Begins

Story of Adam and Lilith

Earth continued to tilt on its axis along with more changes in its energy. At this point, the Eunuch learned of a world that exists within "Ki". Boarding their ships, they left their "Garden City" on the continent of Tampaurban, and traveled to this inner world called, 'Panjia', and they lived there for about the next 70,000 years unknown to the people on the surface of the Earth.

Underneath the Earth, the Eunuchs continued their experiments by re-working the

DNA patterns from the first attempts of their earlier hybrids, and attempting to alter their DNA patterns to create another civilization. When they were finished, their second race proved to be much more successful than their first attempt, but they knew that they still had more to do to establish the perfection of humanoid-humans of male and female.

This led to the second creation of hybrid-humans. But, this time, the Eunuch's used their own technology of Cryogenics to help them to create them.

This time, Adam and Lilith lived in peace and harmony for a long time until, again, they began drifting apart. As before, whenever Adam wished to lie with her, she took offence at the recumbent position, demanding of him:

"Why must I lie beneath you?" she asked. "I also was made in the same manner as you were, and I am therefore your equal."

As Adam tried to compel her obedience by force, Lilith, in a rage, uttered the magic name of God, and then she rose into the air, leaving Adam.

"I have been deserted by my mate that you have created for me," Adam complained to God.

God immediately sent three Angels known as Senoy, Sansenoy, and Semangelof, to find, and bring back Lilith. They found her beside the Red Sea, which was a region abounding in lascivious demons. Again, she bore ***Iiim*** (Demon-Children) at the rate of more than one hundred a day.

"Return to Adam without delay," the angels demanded of her when they found her. "If you do not, we will drown you!'

"How can I return to Adam and live like an honest housewife, after my stay beside the Red Sea?" she asked them.

"It will be death to refuse!" they answered.

"How can I die?" Lilith asked, yet again. "God has ordered me to take charge of all newborn children from the boys up to the eighth day of life when they are circumcised, and girls up to the twentieth day? Nevertheless, if ever I see your three names, or likenesses, displayed in an amulet above a newborn child, I promise to spare it."

To this they agreed, but God still punished Lilith by making one hundred of her demon children perish on a daily basis. [Alpha Beta diBen Sira, 47; Gaster, MGWJ, 29 (1880), 552 ff] Furthermore, he decreed that if she could not destroy a human infant, because of her bargain with the three angels regarding the amulet, she would turn against her own with spite. [Num. Rab. 16.25]

170,000 -110,000 BCE

During this time period, life forms on the surface of Earth begin to experience a metamorphosis stage that merged Spirit and Physical bodies together. The life forms that existed on this planet were of mammals, reptilians, along with the first humanoid-humans.

During this stage, all beings of physical and non-physical form fell into a deep sleep, and their memories of their prior life regarding their technology, was forgotten and turned off, but their building structures remained intact. From this change, came forth a being of a new race, which is known as one of the pre-human races with the combination of having a spirit<>soul. When reawakening to start their new life, they found themselves in a place with no memory and no knowledge about these massive cities, so they moved away from them beginning anew in their new cities that were built in another place.

Since they were created through the means of the use of Cryogenics, they had no belly buttons, but all their offspring did, and they lived thousands of years.

100,000 years ago "Ki", or "Terra", had tilted when pole reversal happened. This changed the planet, and its energy patterns. Pole reversal causes violent Earthquakes, large sleeping

Volcanoes to explode. Movement of large massive bodies of ocean waters changed places with dry land burying civilization after civilization. The ice dome cracked sealing all beings within the inner world, while a massive, inner world flood occurred as the shattered ice and water came rushing into the inner world of Panjia. This, effectively, sealed Panjia, and its inner inhabitants for 50,000 years. By the time they were able to emerge, the Eunuchs had told countless stories, to their creations. Over time, they met with the earlier hybrid of humanoid-humans, as well as all other hybrids.

Thus, the second attempt at human creation ends, and while it was more successful, they continued, but this ended the second story of Adam and Lilith…

Chapter 3

The 3rd Story of Adam and Eve

Eventually, the Eunuchs returned to the continent of Tampaurban and their city stretching one hundred miles around a Mountain in the Ruwenzori Mountains. In the center, the pyramids, temples, and their cities built 100,000 years earlier, still stood. Their technology is intact, but turned off, and not available immediately. After reactivating it, again, the Eunuchs try to alter DNA to create even a more magnificent Human that will surpass all of their past attempts of human creations. But, this time, their goal was to not create a hybrid species, but one that was superior to all others. It is 28,000 BCE, and the Eunuchs are ready to create their third, hybrid humanoid-human race.

Time marched on in Tampaurban, and the Eunuchs, finally, created the perfect human beings through Cryogenics along with altering DNA patterns over 172,000 years. When the time came to awake this race of human beings, they were nude, and in stasis - a deep sleep. Placing these new humans in four groups of twenty-eight, the Eunuchs separated the four groups, and relocated them around the farthest outskirts of the mountain. Keeping them from the inner confines of the city, one day passes. All the humans awaken and marvel at their male and female forms. Time passes, and these new humans begin to establish their own first civilizations.

Meanwhile, the Eunuchs flourish in the lush fertile land with its four waterfalls, which creates four rivers, or **"The Garden of Eden"**

A year has passed. In one of the groups, one of the females decided to journey alone on a path that heads into the forest where a single mountain can be seen in the distant with its magnificent waterfalls cascading to the valley where they live.

After walking on this path for a day, she comes across a building that she has never seen. Approaching the building, she comes across a being that is similar, but different. He looks like her and everyone else back in her village, but he is different in appearance in many different ways. However, they enjoy an exchange of love as they merge as one.

"Who are you?" as she asks in her soft voice.

The being greets her with the two guttural voices of Male and Female.

"Well look at you. How well you have grown!"

"Do you know who I am?" she asks.

"Yes. My race knows who you are. We ask that you return to your village, and bring back whom you embrace and love in the other form. When you return, we will explain all to both of you."

Doing as he asked, she returns to her village. As she enters, she seeks the one who loves and embraces her.

Finding him, she points to the mountain.

"I met another being on them mountain. He asked me to return, and bring the being that embraces me. Will you to come with me?" she asks.

Returning in the same manner taking another day, they arrive at the building. This time, several of these beings were present, and five sit on a bench next to the building. The human female asks a question.

"You told me that you know who I am."

"Yes, I did. But, what we are going to tell you will change your life forever. We are called, Eunuchs. We created you in our image, but as male and female, and you are you are called humans. There were many earlier creations, and over 100,000 years, they spread across this planet - a world we call, 'Ki'."

"What are our names?" she asks.

"We did not give you names. That is your choice. You may pick any name, and we have a list from which you may choose."

Continuing, the Eunuchs tell them about embracing love and that sex between them will create more offspring. That they will continue the procreation of the human race.

"I would like us to be called Eve," she decides.

"And, I would like the name, Adam," he adds.

Adam and Eve began their adventure, and the Eunuchs began recording their journey. And, thus, the conflict of teaching, as well as learning, the knowledge of life to others begins. The information they imparted to them included love, human creation, the stars, and all other life forms throughout the stars.

Throughout ages of the human race, we have wanted to obtain more and more knowledge of the stars and the possibility of other beings. That these beings may have been responsible for humans' existence has been sought for eons. There is no doubt that other beings have had influence over humans, and the Universal Knowledge of Life. In some cases, some did not want humans to know about the truth, so they provided disinformation to them creating fear and terror in order to keep them from knowing the truth.

Samael and Lilith

Jacob and Isaac were two brothers. Their mystical writings reveal that Samael and Lilith were in the shape of an androgynous being. They were double-faced, born out of the emanation of the Throne of Glory and corresponding in the spiritual realm to Adam and Eve, who were likewise born as a hermaphrodite. The two twin androgynous couples resembled each other and both "were like the image of Above - GOD"; that is, that they are reproduced in a visible form of an androgynous deity.[55]

Another version that was also current

among Kabbalistic circles in the Middle Ages establishes Lilith as the first of Samael's four wives: Lilith, Naamah, Igrath, and Mahalath. Each of them are mothers of demons and have their own hosts and unclean spirits in no number.

The marriage of Samael and Lilith was arranged by "Blind Dragon", who is the counterpart of "the dragon that is in the sea". Blind Dragon acts as an intermediary between Lilith and Samael:

Blind Dragon rides Lilith the Sinful -- may she be extirpated quickly in our days, Amen! -- And this Blind Dragon brings about the union between Samael and Lilith. And just as the Dragon that is in the sea (Isa. 27:1) has no eyes, likewise Blind Dragon that is above, in the likeness of a spiritual form, is without eyes, that is to say, without colors.... (Patai81:458) Samael is called the Slant Serpent, and Lilith is called the Tortuous Serpent.[57]

The marriage of Samael and Lilith is known as the "Angel Satan" or the "Other God," but it was not allowed to last. To prevent Lilith and Samael's demonic children from filling the world, God castrated Samael. In many 17th century Kabbalistic books, this mythologem is based on the identification of "Leviathan the Slant Serpent and Leviathan the Torturous Serpent" and a reinterpretation of an old Talmudic myth where God castrated the male

Leviathan and slew the female Leviathan in order to prevent them from mating and thereby destroying the earth.[58] After Samael became castrated and Lilith was unable to fornicate with him, she left him to couple with men who experience nocturnal emissions. A 15th or 16th century Kabbalah text states that God has "cooled" the female Leviathan, meaning that he has made Lilith infertile and she is a mere fornication.

The 4th Story of Adam and Eve

The 4th story is the most known story to us today which was told age after age. In the Bible, Genesis is the account of the creation of Human Race through Adam and Eve. But this story is symbolical both in nature and in life. Or, is it all or has it been changed to protect the truth from the human race?

The story details with both positive and negative aspects. The Tree of Life, used as a positive icon, and The Tree of Knowledge used as a negative icon, and to ingrain fear. It was fine to eat of the fruit of The Tree of Life, while it was forbidden to eat of the fruit of The Tree of Knowledge. When told not to do something, mankind, typically, does so anyway despite having been warned. Adam and Eve are also represented as good and evil - or positive and negative energies, yet many have missed the knowledge.

The Book of Genesis contains dual creation accounts, and was misinterpreted as well. Genesis 2:22 describes God's creation of Eve from Adam's rib, yet is indicative that another woman had been made.

"So God created man in his own image, in the image of God created he him; male and female created he them."

The text places Lilith's creation after God's words in Genesis 2:18 that "it is not good for man to be alone". As I have described earlier, Lilith, like Adam, was formed from the same clay. Lilith claims that since she and Adam were created in the same way, they were equal, and she refuses to submit to him.

Adam asked God to bring Lilith back to him, sending angels to take her back.

"Leave me!" she said. "I was created only to cause sickness to infants. If the infant is male, I have dominion over him for eight days after his birth, and if female, for twenty days."

When the angels heard Lilith's words, they insisted she go back. But she swore to them by the name of the living and eternal God:

"Whenever I see you, your name, or see your forms on an amulet, I will have no power over that infant."

She also agreed to have one hundred of her children die every day. Accordingly, every day, one hundred demons perished. This is the reason that we write these angels' names on the amulets of young children. When Lilith sees their names, she remembers her oath, and the child recovers.

Chapter 4

Story #2 of the 4th creation

"According to Hebrew legend, Lilith was also the first woman God created as a companion for Adam (Graves and Patai's Hebrew Myths and Reuther's Womanguides). Of course, Adam and Lilith differed anatomically, because the Bible refers to a male as one who "pisseth against the wall" [1 Sam. 25:34; 1 Kings 14:10; 21:21]). When Lilith objected to having to lie beneath Adam during sexual intercourse, she was describe in rabbinic tradition as a "baby-killing demoness" who seduces sleeping men. Lilith is mentioned in Isa. 34:14, while the KJV describes her as a "screech owl".

According to a Hebrew tradition, cited in Graves and Patai, God allowed Adam to watch while He created a second woman. The process of creating her, so disgusted Adam, he found her repulsive even though she was beautiful, and God sent her away. So, in our most familiar of stories, while Adam slept, Yahweh created the Eve from Adam's rib that we all know which is found in Genesis. God presented her to Adam, who said happily, “this is now bone of my bones, and flesh of my flesh: she shall be called Woman, because she was taken out of Man” (Gen. 2:23)."

Story #3 of the 4th creation

Early theologians had a real problem with the status of women in regard to Genesis. They believed that she was a weak creature who could twist Adam around her finger bringing death on the entire human race. Their “logical” answer resulted in they presented Eve by splitting her into the Madonna/whore dichotomy. There is a Biblical basis for Lilith.

Genesis 1:27: “So, God created man in his own image, in the image of God he created him; male and female he created them.”

In Genesis 2, Adam is created first and Eve is an afterthought to appease his loneliness. Because of this, many view it as evidence that Adam had two wives. Lilith was the first, but refused to become pregnant. Some traditions say that she was impregnated, then bore demons to him. The evidence for this is the statement in Genesis 5:3: “Adam begat a son in his image” giving the implication that there had been sons not in his image.

Even today, some parents will charcoal a

magic circle with the words “Adam and Eve baring Lilith” on the wall near their babies, as well as the names of the angels on the door.”

Some say God let Adam try making a woman after Lilith, but the creation was so horrible God destroyed it before giving it life. A particularly amusing Victorian story claims a dog ran off with Adam's rib, devoured it before God found him, so Eve was made using one of the dog's ribs.

A mythological story claims that Lilith was an immortal simply because she never ate of the Tree of the Knowledge of Good and Evil. She was also rewarded for service by Asmodeus, the demon of lechery, luxuriousness, as well as evil revenge, and she, now, rules one of the levels of Hell in the company of Namah, Machlath, and Hurmizah. Her power is still over newborn children and women in childbirth. She may take boys up to the eighth day and girls up to the twentieth if she so wishes. She is also the mother of the Lilim, or Lilot, the Djinn, and the succubui and incubi. Other Biblical references of Lilith are:

Isaiah 34:14 - “night hag” (NIV translates this as “Desert creatures” and “night creatures”. In Psalm 91, she is called “terror by night”.

Story #4 of the 4th creation

The first medieval source to depict the myth of Adam and Lilith in full was the Midrash Abkier (ca. 10th century), which was followed by the Zohar and Kabbalistic writings. Adam is said to be a perfect saint until he recognizes either his sin, or Cain's homicide, that is the cause of bringing death into the world. He then separates from holy Eve, sleeps alone, and fasts for 130 years. During this time Lilith, also known as Pizna or Naamah, desired his beauty and came to him against his will. Accordingly, she bore him many demons and spirits called "the plagues of humankind". The added explanation was that it was through Adam's own sin that Lilith overcame him against his will.

Older sources do not state clearly that after Lilith's Red Sea sojourn, she returned to Adam and begat children from him. In the Zohar, however, Lilith is said to have succeeded in begetting offspring from Adam during their short-lived connubium. Lilith leaves Adam in Eden, as she is not a suitable helpmate for him. She returns, later, to force herself upon him. However, before doing so, she attaches herself to Cain and bears him numerous spirits and demons as well.

Another widely taught version of this is that the Hebrew cosmogony originally told a story of Yahweh creating Adam to marry a local Goddess-associated figure named Lilith. Lilith was a follower of the Great other Goddess, Inanna - later known as both Ishtar and/or Asherah.

In yet another story recounted in The Epic of Gilgamesh, Gilgamesh was said to have destroyed a tree that was in a sacred grove dedicated to the Goddess Ishtar / Inanna /Asherah. Lilith ran into the wilderness in despair, and was depicted in the Talmud and Kabbalah as the first wife to Yahwehs's first creation of man, Adam. In time, as stated in the Old Testament, the Hebrew followers continued to worship "False Idols", like Asherah, as being as powerful as Yahweh. Jeremiah speaks of his (and Yahweh's) displeasure at this behavior of the Hebrew people's worship of the Goddess in the Old Testament. Lilith, subsequently, is discovered to be a demon, and she is banished from Adam and Yahweh's presence, and Eve became Adam's wife. Lilith then took the form of the serpent in her jealous rage at being displaced. Lilith in disguise proceeds to trick Eve into eating the fruit from the Tree of Knowledge causing the downfall of all of mankind. It is worthwhile to note that in religions pre-dating Judaism, the serpent was known to be associated with wisdom and re-birth when it sheds its skin.

The 5th creation 14,000 BCE

Garden of Eden – North of Persian Gulf

God had created the heavens, stars, Earth, and all life within six days. On the seventh day, he rested. "God" created Adam from the dust of the Earth, yet no timeline is given for life within "The Garden of Eden". For an unknown time period, Adam roamed the Earth nude, and was the one and only humanoid being at this time.

A curious question arises.

"Why only create only one male humanoid being to roam this world for an unknown time?"

It is a question that no one seems to be asking, but while one question remains unanswered, another one arises.

"Why do the people not ask that question?"

Continuing, and at some point later, this same male lays down within this lush, yet fertile land of "The Garden of Eden", and is placed into a deep sleep. One of his ribs is removed, and a female is created. Both awaken, nude, marveling at one another's beauty not only of each other, but the world around them. They wander through the Garden, and on one of her own journeys alone, Eve discovers a tree. There was only one warning given to Adam and Eve by God:

"You may eat the fruit of the Tree of Life, but do not eat of fruit from the Tree of

Knowledge, for the day you do, you will surely die."

Other questions arise, but those reading the story still do not ask any questions. Either they are not interested, or they believe the questions are forbidden, since they have been told since youth to never ask questions of the Bible or God. In the tree, another being is present, and is known only as a "serpent" who tells her that she had been lied to, and if she eats of the fruit of the tree, her eyes will be opened to all truth. Going against God's warning, she eats, and bringing Adam to this tree, and enticing him to eat, gives Adam a taste as well. He, too, caves, and eats of the fruit. This "serpent" tells both of them about their true existence - who they are and how they became to be created in their human appearance.

They eat, realize they are naked, and begin to cover themselves with leaves, and later, clothing to hide their nudity. God rebukes them when he realizes that they know they are nude, and punishes them accordingly and banishing them from the Garden forever.

Because they sought knowledge instead of life, God was angry with them. We can only assume this one-sided conversation that may have existed.

"We have asked you upon many times to tell us of who we are and how we were created. In addition, every time that we ask you those questions, you always tell us that you have created us in your image. Then, we ask you to show us what you look like, so we can see for ourselves. Moreover, to this very day, you still refuse to tell us. So we went to the tree to find the questions that you refuse to tell us."

If this is a god of righteousness and of truth, knowledge and wisdom, then why keep all of it from them? Why, should we accept this being as the "God", if all he does is humans for wanting to learn the truth? In fact, this so-called "God" is really the deceiver of Life. Yet we are being told to keep away from all others except for "God".

The story of Adam and Eve continues.

Many of the stories found in the Bible tell us that Adam and Eve are the beginning of "Human civilization". By creating human life, Adam and Eve beget children, and God became furious with them. And, thus, the story of Cain and Abel is among the first known story of murder.

Cain and Abel

After a long and severe conflict, the faithful few decided to dissolve all union with the apostate since they refused falsehood and idolatry. They saw that this separation was an absolute necessity if they would obey the word of the "God". They dared not tolerate fatal errors fatal that would compromise their own souls, nor did they wish to set an example, that would imperil the faith of their children and children's children. To secure peace and unity, they were ready to make any concession vowing fidelity to God. However, they felt that peace would be purchased at the sacrifice of their principles. Therefore, if unity could be secured only by compromising truth and righteousness, then they chose difference - even it meant war.

Therefore, they were hated by the wicked just as Abel was hated by the ungodly Cain. For the same reason that Cain slew Abel, these sought to throw off the restraint of the Holy Spirit by putting to death God's people.

After Cain killed his brother, Abel, his mind became filled with thoughts that were not his. Constant voices invaded Cain's mind, he became distraught when he realized they would not cease, and he left his family. He wandered afar, and spent months of traversing Tampaurban. Since it was half desert, this was laborious. Finally, Cain came across a city with hundreds of people.

But, what is wrong with this picture? Another question must be asked.

If there was only Adam and Eve, then from where did the other people come? Since there is no mention of other human creations within the stories within the bible, then these people must already have been created.

There are many other references all throughout the bible. There must be other stories of other pre-human civilizations other than the one and only story of Adam and Eve. Other things within this Book yields more questions than we name. Even though others tell us to ignore the questions, still, they linger throughout man's history, making no further advancement into the answers that lie just outside of our reach.

Suffice it to speculate that there are far more stories of Human Evolution that are hidden from us.

Or, are they? The stories that are woven in and out of all the different civilizations that have come and gone, and those within the mythology of our world, may be able to help us piece together the truth of our world and our own civilization. As it is, now, all we have are false theories, fatal delusions, which keep others from asking the questions that must be answered!

There are many who are as curious as others - even the followers of Christ. Yet, the ingrained idea that we must never ask questions keeps us just on the outside of a truth that is still kept from us. Surely, it is time for these questions to be asked, and hopefully answered through research as our civilization, and mankind's very existence, continue to be pushed back tens of thousands of years as new and ancient civilizations are still being discovered on an almost daily basis.

Chapter 5

Stories of Battles between Beings of Light and Dark

Noah's Flood 8,000 BCE

The World Flood of Noah is believed to have occurred approximately 10,000 years ago. The Bible does not give us a time-line, so this is a rough estimate based on other sources.

Before the Great Flood, it is explained how the civilization viewed their world. In the Bible, it is said that they "knew not until the flood came, and took them all away; so," in the words of our Savior, "shall also the coming of the Son of man be."

In other words, when the world does not expect anything, the professed people of God will be uniting with the world. They will be living in luxury; participating in forbidden pleasures; the luxury of the church prevails; and when the marriage bells are chiming, the end will come. When they are looking forward to many years of world and personal prosperity, the end will come without warning just as fast as lightning flashes from the heavens, will the truth appear, and their bright visions and delusional hopes will cease. As God sent His servants to warn the world of the coming Floods, so he will send his chosen messengers to warn that the final judgment is at hand. Noah's contemporaries laughed at him, and scorned the predictions of the disaster that was coming to them, so in Miller's day many will laugh at the End Times.

So ends human civilization, and another will arise.

'The people all have been told about of the GOD'S and the DEVIL'S, (Or in other terms, 'The Fallen Ones). For the past 12 Thousand years these stories had been created and been handed down from our past generations of ages ago.'

'These beings of Light and Dark, are merely beings from other worlds that exists amongst the Trillions of Quadrillions of star systems that lies within our Milky Way Galaxy. How can I go about saying something of this nature, when sixty percent of Earth population does not accept that possibility of other life in the Milky Way Galaxy or in any of the other trillion galaxies that is part of our Universe that is seen and unseen?'

'Well, for all Truth and Knowledge are within all of us at all times...'

Prior to the last global flood ten thousand years ago, there is no mention of gods or devils. However, post-flood, these were invented, and people believed for the very simple reason that they *wanted* to believe in them.

What's interesting is that for the past thousand years, an off-world influence infiltrated most of the religions upon Earth. Some of these Alien Beings looked into human thoughts, notating their fears and indoctrinated them into those fears. They created the gods. Like everything else, some were good, some were not, and at least 75% of them enhanced those fears with the most terrifying events humans could imagine. And, once these were embedded into human psychology, then the beings took on the roles of these gods and devils keeping a veil of illusion against the truth. Finding humans highly susceptible, and easy to manipulate, only spurred them forward to add to those illusions as time went on – changing the "rules", so to speak.

As time marched forward, humans were so serious about their gods and devils, they continued their beliefs for thousands of years. Until humans began to gain knowledge quickly from some source altering minds and taking responsibility for the thoughts along with their actions of the past and of the present.

For twelve thousand years, these ancient beings craved our fear. It's what they need to exist. They predicted things that would come, and when they happened, the fear of man caused them to pray for help. What the people did not know was that these same beings of light and dark were the same group of beings, and that they were also engaged in battles with many other beings. Their only desire was to "play" with mankind, and cared not for their well-being, but only for their own.

They use several different ways to force the human population to believe. To keep the fears at their height, they used natural world changes such as the weather, portraying them to be a sign of the End Times. Another way was to use war, famine, and disease by pitting humans against humans, and dividing up their religion as well as in politics. Conflicts of thought and belief was critical in keeping humans in line. Today, they have been able to magnify all of these by the technology of today, and most especially through the internet. The hate and evil spreads like wildfire, now, through social media, too.

Those gods and devils have had multiple names through the ages, many with names with which we are familiar. Representing many different things, each god had his/her own area of "expertise". For instance, Ares/Mars was the god of war. Aphrodite/Venus was the goddess of love. Remember...each of these being used their forces to keep humans in fear, or happiness. Pitting one against the other. Of course, the two main gods were Hades/Pluto and the top of these beings was Zeus/Jupiter. As always, again, evil and good. While this was their representations, the truth was that they cared nothing whatsoever for humans, and what caused mankind to dispense with them was that very reason when they realized that these "gods" cared nothing for us. Once we stopped believing in them, they lost their power of fear over us. Or did they? Perhaps they have not yet stopped considering wars, disease, famine, and all other things still occur. Perhaps they still influence us with stories such as Armageddon where there will be one final battle between light and dark? It does seem that we hear more bad than good.

Mankind is notorious for never wanting to accept responsibility for their own actions, and therefore, these beings easily influence us even today. With the truth staring at us, we are told that if we do not obey them, we will go to "Heaven or Hell" or "The Void".

The deities, with which we so deem them, read our thoughts of our needs, fears, and everything else. They were actually playing roles they had created for themselves simply by reading human thoughts, and extrapolating from our fears, needs, and even love. And, they did so perfectly...so much so that even though they departed three-thousand years ago, we still believe they exist, and still wait for "The End Times", and believe that they will save us.

But, what else can we find in our stories that will tell us exactly what these beings have done? Is it possible we have some tangible proof if we can just discover it?

The most powerful, and famous of all devices, was...

"The Ark of the Covenant"

The deities seemed to like to present mankind with devices of their making, giving man instructions on how to build them. The Ark of Noah was an amazing feat for a man who had no experience whatsoever building a boat. Yet, he was given a set of very specific instructions on how to build this massive ship. And, on top of that, it was to carry two of every kind of animal in the world! He was told that they would come to him, and he would place them aboard the Ark in order to survive the flood.

But, the most famous of all devices is the one that had more power than any other. And, that was, of course, "The Ark of the Covenant". The very specific instructions on how to build this device was imperative to keep men from being killed by just touching it! Specific instructions such as the wood, how much gold to overlay, the angels with the wings, and even the poles that were to carry the Ark by only specific people dressed in specific types of clothing, attested that this was a huge device of power. Men did approach it without the correct clothing, or rituals, and they died. But, is it real? And, if so, then where is it? There are many placed on Earth that boast that they have the Ark, but as of right now, there is no proof it still exists. However, many people still believe it does, and has fueled many with the desire to find it – to possess the power it represents.

The Ark of the Covenant can be seen here between the pillars on the left of picture

Other stories come to mind as well: “David and Goliath”, the boy who brought down a giant, and became King of Nation, and the ancestor to Jesus Christ; “Sodom and Gomorrah”, the twin cities who were completely destroyed by God in a blast so big, He warned Lot and his family what would happen if they looked back, while his wife did, and became a pillar of salt; “Gilgamesh”, a demi-god whose legend and myth eerily almost mirrors the story of Noah: "The Tower of Babel" in Babylon, which was the last time mankind had a common language, and the beginnings of all our countries of today were formed. And, of course, the final battle of all – Armageddon where good will fight evil on Earth.

There is a definite pattern to these stories, and interestingly enough, all these stories take place in the countries of the Middle East even until today. In today's world, though, they have involved every nation in the world with their fight. In essence, the last war of Earth will consist of all nations.

Beings of Ancient Times

Our minds have been flooded with all sorts of these stories, but there are pictures of these ancient beings giving us a "visual record" in the representation of the way the people saw them in ancient days. These pictures are available in ancient cave, or temple drawings. The most famous of these drawings show both beings with horns as well as beings with wings. Of course, these were given the names "Devil" and "Angel", respectively. Those with the horns became infinitely evil where those with wings were visualized as good, and eventually given the name of “angel”.

Male and Female winged beings were called, “Zephyrs”, or Angels, and appear in the Bible. These were associated with “Angels” by our human ancestors, and that word has been consistent since that time.

Other beings within our mythology have also appeared. Satyrs were a being of half-man, half-goat, and was insatiable for women and sex. Others, such as the Centaur, a being of half-man, half-horse created from two warring factions. Another was half-man, half-fish, or Merman, who was known as Poseidon, and appears in many ancient myths, and even in the story of the Lost Island of Atlantis. Even the Bible makes mentions of some of these odd halves.

Mankind also has some very real fears of very real animals. Reptiles are rarely seen as "good" in any species such as snakes, lizards, crocodiles, iguanas', and many others. Of all the species on the Earth, this one group not only can live on land, but they also can live in fresh water as well as salt water. They are identified by scales over their body, which makes them hard to hurt or kill. Of course, that is no longer true with today's tools, but there was a time when they were almost immortal throughout their own lifespans. While this encompasses most all reptiles, there are a few exceptions such as the turtle with whom we truly have a fondness even to the point of parking our cars on the road, and picking them up carrying them to the other side keeping them from getting killed by a car. And, in some cases, tiny lizards that skitter quickly across our yards, but bother no one. I guess we are fickle about reptiles in a way!

But, there is also another theory. That we come from a reptilian race of beings. Or, perhaps some of us come from reptilian ancestors. Knowing our fears of reptiles, and their cousins, serpents, are we misplacing our fears?

Reptilian beings are of the constellation, "Draco"

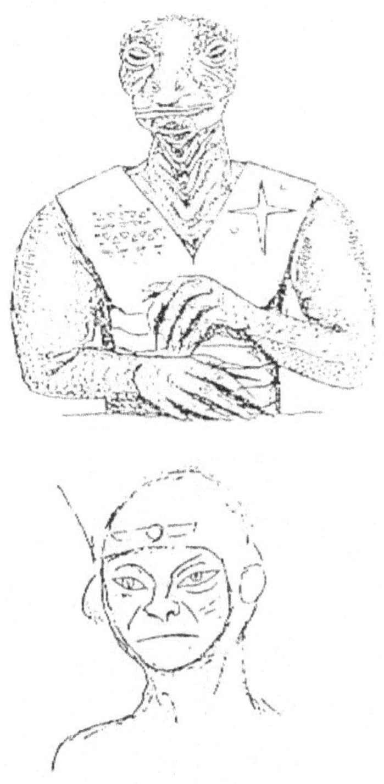

Serpent beings are of the constellation, "Ophiuchus"

Both of these beings represent positive beings, not the negative aspects that religions are making these beings out to be. These beings been around for well over 300,000 years, and come from many star systems around our galaxy. Some Reptilian's come from the Sirius Star system, and some are from the Orion star system. Still others come from the star system of Draco, while the some of the Serpent beings are from the star system of Ophiuchus, and other systems in the Universe as well.

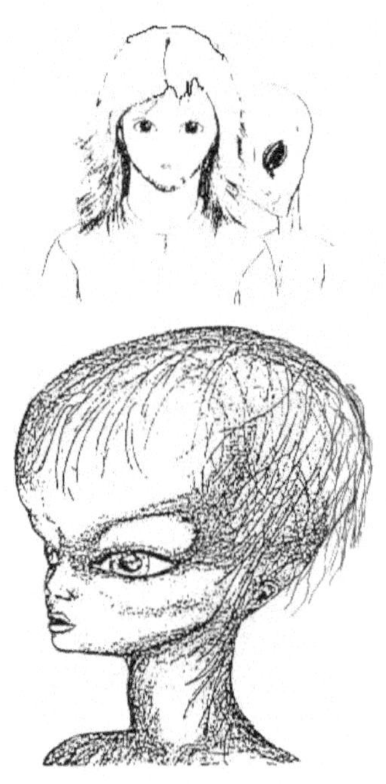

Another being that most of us are truly familiar with are the "aliens" which have been associated with kidnapping humans. The most famous of these incidents was the crash in Roswell, New Mexico in 1947.

Beings called the "greys", or less known,

"Delphis", and were created from several star groups known as, "Zate Reticuli 1 & 2" and "Delphium", which are within our own Milky Way Galaxy that can be seen our night sky. These hybrid beings are of the next generation, which are of the combination of several genetics of DNA strands, including human DNA, from many species from across the universe. These "greys" we have heard about only in recent years. Maybe in about another 20 plus years we might meet these hybrid beings that will be a new race of beings on this world.

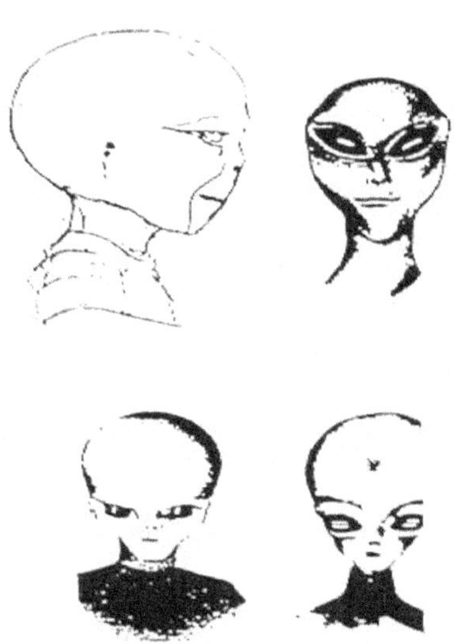

These are four types of many of the Delphi's (known as the Greys).

The drawings of the typical, Yeti, Bigfoot, and are also known as the Lemurian Beings.

Along with Atlantis, another ancient landmass existed called Lemuria. Some believe that it existed at the same time as Atlantis, and sunk at the same time as well. The Lemurians, survivors of Lemuria's sinking, are better known by their common names of today: Yeti, Bigfoot, etc. This ancient race of beings is the survivors of an ancient race from Lemuria. These beings existed over 200,000 years. In addition, they are widely read about in pre-ancient myth. In addition, yes, they are also known throughout our current culture as well, but you call them by many names based on their locations around the world today. You call them the Yeti, Bigfoot and by many other names.

These beings had moved into their quantum leap into consciousness around 25,000 years ago and they are multidimensional beings, they exists in our world around us, but in the sixth dimensional world. These beings also have telepathic ability for communication to those that are able to communicate telepathically. And yes they come into our dimension at times, which is to say, to check up on us in a way of speaking that is, since we too are moving from our 3rd dimensional existence and entering into the 4th and 5th dimensional existence. Which we will be seeing more of these beings in the near future.

"One might ask, why are these beings of these other star systems interested in us, and why have they been watching over our star system and planet?"

The one reason is that we are their brothers and sisters. We are on this earth as many forms of species, not all life is based on the human species. Most people cannot come to believe in that there is other life besides ours in this galaxy that we are in, that there are other beings; that exists off Terra. All you have to do is look around you, there is other species of life besides humans, which there are other life forms which are more intelligent that the human species is, by thousands of time more, which is mainly because these species are thousands of years older than, our current human species statutes is. The other reason for the return of some ancient beings back to our star system is that our star system is moving into a new age, a new cycle of life, and a new frequency of energy. I talked about that from the very beginning with book 1(The Reawakening), and throughout this whole series! Yes everything – everyone, is moving forward on the ladder of evolution on consciousness. Some and I mean only a hand full has already moved forward into this consciousness of Reawakening and those that are beginning to awake to come to the realization of Who They Are as a conscious beings. Some of these star beings are here on our request and some of the other beings are here to observe the transition of all species that are on the earth as we all enter into our new beginning of this new cycle of life. As we reawaken, that knowledge that is lies within all of us as we come to the realization and the understanding of who we are as conscious beings. These beings from the stars are paving the way in front of all of us, they are the way showers, they ask for those beings that are on this world that had already reawakened to assist them in helping the rest of the beings on Terra that had not awakened yet!

These ancient beings that were on our world several thousands of years ago, which are returning to Terra system, from those far off stars that these beings are coming from. As all of you might recall in those ancient stories, which are part of our mythology stories as you call them. All those beings had always been interacting with this star system from millions of years and will continue to do so, when the beings of this star system request their interactions. Or these star beings will take it upon themselves to interact with the inhabitants of a planet based on the changes of the cycle, energy frequency that a star system is entering into.

On the other hand, if a being is needed to be placed on the planet to help influence the people to change before the new cycle begins. But for us at this new age, that we are entering which began as of the year 2000 which was paved before us 2000 years ago, on that reawakening of who we truly are. In addition, it has taken this long, but that was only due to our past age that ended back in 1985.

The galaxy that we are in is finally moving

forward into a new beginning, a new age, this also goes for all beings as well that is within this galaxy. We all are leave the past age, that old energy and moving into a very new frequency, as I mentioned earlier and within Book 1. This is also, why the interest in these stars systems and all the beings, in this sector of this galaxy. Which is to observe all life and to see if they are reawakening and realizing, who they are, as conscious beings and to see if you are ready to move and to take that quantum leap into consciousness. As I said earlier only a hand full, had already came to the understanding of who they are as conscious beings. For those that had already reawakened are not controlled by the so called god theory of those religions, this hand full is about 5 % plus of the human species and that is pretty small hand full to say the least. This is why that this request from those awakened beings upon your planet, they had put out the call for the assistance on the help of paving the way, to help all beings on your planet to realize, who each and every one of you are. So you can become aware of, who you are and taking that next step of evolution!

What part do the ones that are called, 'The Fallen Ones', has a role in our lives?

Thought can be used to control, destroy, it can be used as well to create at the same time. From one Being's Thought, creates life, so can another Being's Thought can be used to control of another Being's life.

How did this come about? Well, some say in the Beginning! Well, there is never a Beginning "It just appears to look like a Beginning from a perspective, A view point of one's own life on where they were brought into existence," This is a never ending circle of life. As all Being's come to realize, at one point or another, that all Beings that are existing, are realizing their own thoughts, were being created in front of them, as well, as for the so called first Being's Thought was being created, at the same time. So, since this cycle of life going from, beginning through its destruction than back into being created again, 'who is to say, there is only one Being that can create upon the mere Thought of creating and or destroying.' This is everyone's thought. The Thought, that creates one's own existence. The Thought that creates another one's thought into existence. Which also, brings forth the creation of the Beings, to go with the Thoughts?

In this instance, brings forth the beginning moments of these Beings, that will exist for the experience of that thought for this creation, that they all took part in, bringing these thoughts, and all those Beings of positive, negative into reality, of what may seem to be past, present and of the future. All these Beings react to, other Beings thoughts, and they help create the world(s) around them. Based on all the Thoughts that are being put out around them, some of these Beings will come to see these Beings as of good (positive) Evil (negative). In addition, for those, so called Beings of good and evil, are in a way, stuck in playing this so called creation, based upon, the other Beings that brought this thought into creation.

So, you have the Beings that created the Thought, in the past, which, is now, being experienced, by the very Being that created the Thought without knowing, it was their own thoughts of the past. Which is now, becoming reality for them to experience their own creation is now their worst nightmare? Because, they are not aware it is their own Thoughts that they are experiencing, in the present. All of the, good (creation) and evil (destruction) that these Beings feared and thought of in the past, is now their experiences. These Beings had gone about creating a "god, Thought, a Being," for all the Beginning (creation) and of good. Along with a Being of "evil, end of all things, (destruction). Some of, These Beings, "The People," of today, are realizing that they created all of these experiences that we all are going through. While the other 75% are still going about thinking, that some other, Beings, if it be a (god or some devil), that created this experience, that we are going through.

These people are now, creating a new Thought of the End, of what may play out, with these Two Beings of light and dark. Along with what these Two Beings may appear as. However, they also gone about fearing, as these Beings and the experiences if it were good or bad, as they feared the experiences, of what they just witnessed, of the past.

These people have more to fear than, those two Beings that were created by their own Thoughts. They have the fear of the thoughts of all Beings that exists.

Thoughts of positive and negative energies have always been in existence from age to age. It is the more current age that all Beings fear. Because, they created these so called Beings, to represent, the Thoughts, of positive and negative aspects of all there thought. Therefore, you have many, Beings that are representing, good (positive) and evil (negative).

All this was brought on, around 7,000 BC mainly, because, the people did not want to be held accountable for their Thoughts and Actions.

Now, we are living in a time, that we all must understand, the thoughts that brought these, so called Beings, into existence. Which represents, the good and evil as being part of us all? And, totally come to terms, it is us, and we are these Beings of good and evil, that we created, to take this blame, the burden, from us, so we can blame our life on these beings of good and evil.

Therefore, one thought, ushers in the creation, of life, (which you are the creator of life, the one that Thought it), which all, that will witness, as being created by some Being'(s)? Therefore, the one's that ends up witnessing these events, are saying, "that a Being of wonderful powers, brought these events, creations, into manifestation, or foretold of what will come to be." Without realizing, it was ourselves in the past that, Thought of the events of the future, that all of us, would come to experience, in time. All of us, created all of these god'(s) and devil'(s) in the past. Which most of you, will come to fear, your own creations as we nearer the future? Which these events are to come about?

We all are taking part in, creating all the faces of good and evil, light and dark, god'(s) and devil'(s), which are no more than only positive and negative aspects of one's own self.

However, if there was only Adam and Eve, then from where did the other people come? Since there is no mention of other human creations within the stories within the bible, then these people must already have been created.

There are many other references all

throughout the bible. There must be other stories of other pre-human civilizations other than the one and only story of Adam and Eve. Other things within this Book yields more questions than we name. Even though others tell us to ignore the questions, still, they linger throughout man's history, making no further advancement into the answers that lie just outside of our reach.\

Suffice it to speculate that there are far more stories of Human Evolution that are hidden from us.

Or, are they? The stories that are woven in and out of all the different civilizations that have come and gone, and those within the mythology of our world, may be able to help us piece together the truth of our world and our own civilization. As it is, now, all we have are false theories, fatal delusions, which keep others from asking the questions that must be answered!

There are many who are as curious as others - even the followers of Christ. Yet, the ingrained idea that we must never ask questions keeps us just on the outside of a truth that is still kept from us. Surely, it is time for these questions to be asked, and hopefully answered through research as our civilization, and mankind's very existence, continue to be pushed back tens of thousands of years as new and ancient civilizations are still being discovered on an almost daily basis.

Chapter 6

Evolution of the Next Humans

Most humans fear what they do not understand. Because of this, we live in denial that within this galaxy, as well as others, other *intelligent* lifeforms exist. Humans prefer consistency and that which is normal. When the unexplainable enter our real world, humans want scientist to "explain" it, but they are not really wanting it explained. Therefore, Science is used to disprove anything that cannot be explained by something that is normal within our world, and our concept of normal. If the vast majority of Scientists say something is, then it is. Even if they do know the truth, or just simply "ignore" it, they believe humans are not capable of the truth.

What we really need to know is why are the "Star Beings" even interfering in our evolution?

Our mythology is the proof of these "Star Beings", and they have been shown by ancestors leaving us depictions in caves, and copying other depictions within ancient manuscripts. They are constant and consistent with consistency being the key. These stories were first based upon repetition in the form of bards long before writing was invented. Bards were people who were in almost every culture who were charged with the preservation of their own culture. The stories they told over and over became legend, and finally mythology. But, almost every culture on this planet preserved these stories. Were they embellished through the ages? Of course, but the basic stories, while the names are different, are far too much alike to not be true. We must rip the embellishments away in order to see the truth of the stories. These beings have been here from the first. They are real.

The past age ended for humans in 1985, and we entered the new age in 2000 paved 2000 years ago for us. Our galaxy is moving forward into a new beginning and a new age. Most of us "feel" this end, although the majority ignore it, because they refuse to believe it, and the skeptics – especially in the scientific area – have convinced them it is not true. Over the last 60 years, space has opened to us in ways we never could imagine except within our culture of science fiction. Now, though, science fiction has become science fact. And, even though humans accept this, most still refuse to believe that we are not alone – we never have been. While UFO's have been present in all of our history, never have they been more numerous since World War II. They have been observing us; waiting for enough to awaken so that they can proceed to the next evolutionary stage of humans.

There are many who have awakened to this. The very fact that mainstream science is being flooded with questions by them attests to this. 5% of humans are cognizant of it, and more are coming to the truth since 2000. These are no longer controlled by either religion or science. Now, they think independently. The “star beings” have come simply because their monitoring shows the increased energy of the human's minds. The next evolution is on its way.

“The Fallen Ones”, for those who do not know, were angels who were banished from heaven to Earth for following Lucifer who desired to rule in God's place. Their role is through “thought” which can be used to control, destroy, and even create simultaneously.

From a human standpoint, “The Beginning” is where to start. But, that is because we *limit* our minds to a beginning, and even an end. However, there is no beginning or end, but it is a never ending circle of life. In other words, thought is actually a paradox! However, in this instance, these “Star Beings” worked together for the experience to bring both positive and negative thought to our current Universe and our planet, Earth. And, frankly, to all intents and purposes, “The Fallen” are “stuck” on Earth, and are also a part of this thought. Their influence on humans is unprecedented with evil. But, thoughts of good are equally as strong on humans as well. Both are competing for these, and yet, they have no choice in what we decide. This is why humans have choice to be good or evil.

It is the thoughts of humans of the past that have a direct result of our thoughts of today, and because this, we have created our own worst nightmares! Awareness of our own thoughts is almost non-existent, and therefore, we do not realize that our ancestors' thoughts were directly from the "Star Beings", but our own imaginations have developed into disbelief of all but that which science or religion tells us is truth. Not everything is passed on by those who went before us. Whether that is by design, or ignorance, is a moot point. And, that is why an "End" of our very existence through war is beginning to emerge – the thought that the "End" is the one thing that has been professed since the thought of the "Beginning" emerged, and because we believe it, it just may come to pass.

Created around 7000 BC, people then, as today, do not want to be held accountable for their thoughts and actions. This has been a legacy of mankind that even we cannot escape. The problem is that it is we who are responsible for good and evil. It is we who have created beings of good and evil to absolve our own responsibility. Mankind always needs to have someone else to blame for our own actions and thoughts. We witness these events, and blame a higher power.

"Creation of "The Fallen"

Digging ever deeper into the world of religion since 1979, I have come across a very interesting story. There are fifteen volumes of books from The Zoroastrian religions. The fourth book of the The Denkard is composed from sentences selected from Ayinin Amuk Vazin by Adurfarnbag I Farroxzadan, who was the leader of the faith of the family of the educated-in-the-faith and saintly Adarbad Mahraspandan. I have the entire fifteen-volume book of this story, and this story dates from 4,000-1,000 BCE. It is a religion opposed to demons and is the ordinance of Ohrmazda.

Quotes from The Denkard follow:

I make obeisance to Mazda-worshipping religion which is opposed to the demons (and) is the ordinance of Ohrmazda. The matter of the fourth book (of the Denkard) is composed from sentences selected from Ayinin Amuk Vazin by Adurfarnbag I Farroxzadan, the leader of the faith of the family of the educated-in-the-faith, and saintly Adarbad Mahraspandan.

Be it known that the One God is the cause of the beginning (of creation) and is the causer of causes. Cause is not for him (i.e. He is uncaused.)

Among those connected with (God) the second as the second (if we regard Ohrmazda as the first), (and) first among the original creation is Vohuman. The commencement of creation was with Vohuman. The origin adverse to him (i.e. Vohuman's adversary) is (Ahriman) the blemish giving cause of the creation.

Seeing with complete vision (i.e. on careful inquiry) it is found that the other with the perverse understanding (i.e. Ahriman) conducts things in this world (in the path of evil). At times, several original (creations) are destroyed through him. Because his creation separates itself from those how has a close connection with their original master (i.e. God) has taken the side of his adversary. In addition, it is become unfit by not caring to keep up with their connection with their true god and by harming the moderate party (of God) it is broken (from its own party). For the same reason that substance, which is on the adverse side of harming the side (of god) is not fit to receive the gifts (of God). Again, a substance, which has received its life from the one life-giving God, becomes unfortunate through the same cause. Any person who turns against Him from whom he got his birth is not able to improve himself (morally) through his connection with that one (i.e. Ahriman), because he is connected with his (i.e. Ahriman's) substance.

Again that evil one is not, as the creation of Vohuman is, the second creation of God. From this it appears that the great self-existing God who is a law unto Himself is one and alone.

Then from one (creation) after another is created by him. Hence, no one else can be his equal as an adversary (i.e. Ahriman can never equal Him). The one God is He who through that one (i.e., Vohuman) has given birth to innumerable other creations.

The creation connected with that other (i.e. Ahriman) is without religion; how can it be said to have connection with the second (creation, viz. Vohuman)? But that one (i.e. the creation connected with Ahriman) this can be said to be separated from the One (God).

Third-- The creation-increasing origin (i.e. God) keeps the second (creation) Ardwahisht under the supervision of one who is among those connected with Him (i.e. under Vohuman). Among the Amahraspands, Ardwahisht has the third rank. And, he is obedient to the first creation (Vohuman). The reason of this being third (in rank) is that Ohrmazda he is the first and as being the first creation, Vohuman is the second (in rank). And his (i.e. Vohuman's) obedient servants Ardwahisht are considered the third (in rank). From this, Vohuman having obtained his life from Ohrmazda is (Ohrmazda's) obedient servant. And the good custom and law of (men) obeying the authority of Ohrmazda and of living as His obedient servants has (prevailed in the world) from the beginning of creation through the THOUGHT of (Vohuman). Again the good custom of life- possessing men publicly obeying and respecting religious rulers is (prevailing in the world through Vohuman).

Among those connected with the perfect authority of Ohrmazda the fourth in rank called Shahrewar is worthy of being blessed through his possessing life according to Ohrmazda. Moreover, he is a worthy servant of the worker of pure deeds, Ardwahisht. This second (creation, Ardwahisht) is obedient to Vohuman the first creation. (Shahrewar presides over metals. In addition, these give strength for generosity and nourishment to men living a life of piety. Thereby is (acquisition of) honor, (attainment of) one's desires, propagation of the faith, attainment of (both) knowledge and the intuitive wisdom of the good- thought Vohuman. Thereby is the springing up (in the heart) of the desire of obedience to God, the conducting of oneself towards Ardwahisht to one's (own) advantage, and the making one's friends do likewise. To conduct the people by the authority of Ohrmazda and the leadership of the faith is to disgrace the blemish-giver (Ahriman). Moreover, hence the blessed are exalted.

Again he who keeps up the divine religion in this world and rules the people according to the precepts of religion is the (king or priest) the maintainer or religion and of the true and temperate authority of God.

The state through the (inspired) strength of the knowledge of religion is worthy of the trust (of the people) and those who in truth and purity propagate the knowledge of religion among the pious are strong through the strength of the state.

Ungodliness and the intense prevalence of unholy utterances (in state and church) are through the rival efforts of the adversary (i.e. Ahriman) to (keep himself) in touch (with men). In the same way, the method of (men's) speech and deeds is like unto fire. Just as burning fire (first) dries up the wet firewood and (next) after drying up the firewood acknowledges the ruddy light (akin to itself), so too in both ways (i.e. the two referred to above). The people of the world by their holiness are fit to drive away the unholy Druj from among them (i.e. the fire first expels the adverse principle of water from the wet fuel.

So too piety first drives out the unholy element; next the fire makes the fuel glowing hot and absorbs the fuel into itself and so too piety absorbs that which remains after the unholy element has been driven off and makes akin to itself). It behooves the people to acknowledge these obligations to the agents (i.e. the Mobeds and Dasturs) who give them an insight into the nature of the different kinds of Unholiness and those who give rise to different sorts of harms. In the same manner people ought to be always extremely grateful to the good triumphant kings, the defenders of the faith. Because he (i.e. such a king) is the believer in the religion loved of God and more especially because he explains the wisdom underlying the Mazda-worshipping faith. Hence, his good Government is safe and permanent. Then by the adornment derived from his and the Yazad's mutual connection, he is secretly sheltered (and protected). The continuance of his authority one after the other (in his own family) is through divine assistance. Therefore, people should look upon the religious kings who have faith in their religion as courageous, as being the good kings of religion and the kings who are of the law of the (good) faith should attempt to spread in the world the exalted law-abiding wisdom of the Mazda-worshipping faith.

When king Vishtasp became relieved from the war with Arjasp, he sent messages to other kings to accept the (Mazda-worshipping) faith and to spread). Among the people) the writings of the Mazda-worshipping religion which are studded with all wisdom and which relate to the acquisition of knowledge and resources of various kinds, he sent all together (i.e. at the same time). Spiti, Arezrasp and other Mobeds who had studied the languages relating to these (writings) and who had returned from Khwaniras [Xwaniratha] after a complete study of the knowledge of the faith under Frashostar.

Darai son of Darai ordered the preservation of two written copies of the whole *Avesta* and its commentary according as it was accepted by Zartosht, from Ohrmazda, one in the Ganj-i-hapigan and the other in the Dez-i-Napesht.

The Ashkanian government got the *Avesta* and its commentary, which from its (original) pure (and sound) condition had been, owing to the devastation and harm (inflicted by) Alexander and his general of the plundering Ahriman army, separated into parts and scattered about, to be copied out. And any (work) which remained with the Dasturs for their study and the writings subsequently obtained in the city were ordered to be preserved and copies of them to be made out for other cities.

(After this) Ardashir-i-Papakan in his time got a true Dastur named Tosar to arrange together all the scattered writings relating to the *Avesta* and its commentaries. For this (order) Dastur Tosar devoting his attention to (this subject) made one harmonious work after comparison
with other writings. He entrusted the Dasturs with the work of making other copies of it. The king also ordered that other writings relating to the Mazda-worshipping faith with might be obtained after him and of which no information or clue was to be had then should be preserved in the same way.

Shahpuhr son of Ardashir king of kings collected together, from Hindustan, Arum and other places where they had got scattered, writings other than those of the faith (i.e. other than those on prayer, worship, precepts, and law). Such as those relating to medicine, astronomy, geography, minerals, the increase of the glory of life-possessing kinds, the parts of the soul, and (writings relating to) other arts and sciences, and he ordered a correct copy of them after collocation with the *Avesta* to be deposited in the Ganj-i-Shaspigan. In addition, he ordered the (Dasturs and Mobeds) to deliver sermons and speeches to draw the faith of the people without religion to the Mazda-worshipping faith.

Shahpuhr king of kings, son of Ohrmazda warred with the kings of all countries and made them believers in Ohrmazda. He created a taste (for religion) among all people by means of speeches. In addition, he made them investigators of religion. And, at last Adarbad by his admonitions made the people high priest placed before all the non-Zoroastrians an explanation of all the different Nasks of the *Avesta*. Upon which some who accepted the faith confessed to this effect-- we have seen with our eyes every point of the faith and hence every one of us is sure to abandon his evil religion, and we shall keep up our efforts for the faith. Moreover, they did accordingly.

Now Khosraw, king of kings, son of Kobad drove out from among the four divisions of (the people of) the faith (i.e. from the Athonrnan, Artheshtar, Vastriosh and Hutokhsh) any priest of the evil religion and ruler of the evil religion who seemed to be full of enmity to the faith, (in fact he drove out) all these evil men. He has exalted the Zoroastrians (through their faith) by giving them from time to time encouragement and instruction regarding the faith.

Again (Khosraw) has given this order about the (priests gifted with) divine wisdom -- that the clever men who explain the truth of the Mazda-worshipping faith should through their good judgment and foresight encourage the ignorant by teaching them the faith and make them as steadfast as possible in their faith. And the learned supreme high priest, the Dastur of the Dasturs should not enter into religious discussion with the people. However, he should through pure thought, word, and deed is on the side of the good spirits. Moreover, he should piously worship and pray to God through the Manthras that by (his) worshipping with the Manthras we might always call to our mind the leader of our people *i.e.* of the Magus to wit Ohrmazda; The Lord (God) is manifest unto us through spiritual understanding. And the Lord shows us through spiritual **THOUGHT** the measures for our salvation to be understood of us of the world. We will continue to love Him fully from among the Yazad's by both the agencies (of the spiritual and bodily faculties). Moreover, we will continue to remember the Yazad's who work for the prosperity of God's world in order that religious merit might accrue to those of the good faith.

Again, that king (i.e. Khosraw) in an addition to this (work) sent the inhabitants of Iran studding the Mazda-worshipping faith to Khwaniras to study under teachers of exalted wisdom, so that we might acquire full adornment through knowledge of the divine religion. These keep aloof from perverse discussions, exhort (men to lead a good life) through the words of the Avesta and compose books of wisdom. And people through their wise writings keep themselves moderate and honored by obeying those who enlighten them. Again, for this reasons all men regard the Mazda-worshipping faith of divine wisdom as meant for the final existence. Hence, intellectual strangers continue coming to this place (i.e. Iran) for (studying) the Ohrmazda-worshipping divine religion. Explanation of the Mazda- worshipping faith is afforded to people from the outside that continue coming to obtain connection with and zeal for the new religion. The Dasturs after many (religious) researches with still greater zeal travel and instruct those who cannot come there (i.e. to Iran) for the work of obtaining the benefit of the faith.

Again (Khosraw) thus addressed all the Mobeds who are evidently servants of God and of virtuous disposition -- I order you with the best wish (i.e. most sincerely) that you should create a taste for the Avesta and its exposition [Zand] with new and new zeal. By the acquisition of its knowledge (i.e. of the Avesta) the worthy people of the world should be made exalted in rank. They should fully instruct such, as are capable of learning, from among the people of the world, who do not understand the Creator, nor the details regarding his miraculous spiritual creation. Such as are wanting in intelligence and are of perverse THOUGHTS should be instructed in the faith in way that seems best, to wit, by comparisons (and examples) and be who can instruct (people) in the faith with such wisdom should be regarded as the instructing (priest).

The profession of that instructor in the faith, who is a teacher fit for the above (work), who has spiritual gifts, who instructs (men) in every wisdom of the faith and who likewise plainly tells with wisdom the vices of the world to everyone, is the only one which makes men (incline) to the divine faith. He should not expound anything on the authority of the faith, which is not in agreement with the exposition of the faith. Likewise, he should teach on the authority of the faith everything that is found in the faith as a duty he owes to his office.

(The Creator Ohrmazda) for (the maintenance of) His authority produced and gave being to the increase-giving Spandarmad of obedient thought, the fifth among his holy relatives, this is the begetting power for begetting spiritual and earthy creation (in the world). Through Spandarmad is the strength of the earthy body, the sense of feeling, courage and every kind of foresight. Man is obedient to God and possessing His glory because of the presence in him of thought, word, and deed, which makes him obedient to God. For in pious men are the lodgment of the Yazad's for the complete recompense of virtue and the presence of the Yazad's vanishes (from among men) because of their connection with impiety.

Moreover in men is the relation of exalting foresight and five other substances (life, soul, intellect, conscience, and guarding spirit) whose names are mentioned in religion. Ohrmazda created among (His) relatives (i.e. the archangels [Amahraspands]) the essence of (archangel) Hordad sixth in high dignity, always bestowing gifts and endowed with the thought of obedience. This creation on account of its communion with many earthy substances (especially time and water) yields good thought to the good creation in its allotted work, takes proper care of it, as a faith companion keeps itself in communion with the essence of (the good creation,). Then out of the feeling of kinship keeps itself united with (the good creation) to show it the full and proper path in every work and process. In the same manner, the hidden qualities, which are with Hordad -- viz., the resplendent Farohar, conscience, life, intelligence, wisdom, and others pertaining to the affairs of the soul, -- remain as the corrector and manager of the body. The invisible physical senses give intimation unto the soul, of sinful actions, which the body commits with regard to the soul. These invisible (senses) are called the mediators between body and soul. Moreover, these senses yield happiness to both bodies bad souls by making these two assist each other.

The seventh (related to Ohrmazda) is (the Archangel) Amurdad, which, besides yielding protection unto men, always keeps living men immortal and connected with the (faithful) flock.

He is the promoter of thoughtful, meditating nature, bestowed of progeny to the warriors, and begetter of good thought among those who are born. He yields radiance to the bodies of those who are bore good and is of many natures through the mingling of wisdom.

The one existence of God perfects and completes itself in seven (including the sixth spiritual archangels.) It befits all to thank God for perfection in all deed. (As every nature obtains capacity to enjoy life) for being engaged in their proper work, God gets victory (over Ahriman) through the thanks given unto Him by the creatures for being able to occupy themselves in their proper work. This thanksgiving (from men) is due because of the nature they have received from Him (i.e. on account of the useful life obtained from Him.)

Learned archpriests must impart knowledge of religion to the creatures of God. From the scholars of the Manthras-utterances well versed in religion is attained a, proper understanding of the industry each man ought to engage in and of the way he should work.

The creatures are not informed as regards the infinite time connected with God, its nature being understood only by the unique existence (i.e.) the Creator himself.

The creation of finite time on earth is for

(bringing about) the improvement of the creatures having existence by means of a change from one (condition) to another (the change being from the material world, into which man is born from the spiritual, back into the spiritual state.) As regards the cause of creation) it is said in religion that everyone comes into being from Him who has being (i.e. God) and every creature that is created obtains existence from that existent (i.e. God.)

The utterances of God (i.e. the sayings of the Mazdayasnian religion) are a law unto the existing (i.e. to men.) There is nothing without order. Some of the substances are finite. Moreover, the substance wanting in order is from the blemish giver (i.e. is on the side of Ahriman,) and is said to be the substance following the law of wicked similitude. (I.e. of Ahriman) and existing without rule and limit (i.e. without the restriction of law.) Just as the period of the Creator's existence is infinite so is the exalted soul; how can it (ever) have non-existence?

The creation, which is produced, receives by its actions gifts of a high order from God.

Moreover, men perform meritorious actions because of fate or destiny and it is this account of (destiny) that a being of the earth is considered famous among the spiritual Yazad's. Through the performance of actions pertaining to the spiritual world is man's high destiny. In this world, a man of greatness receives the favor of God so long as he has faith in the shining Yazad's. In the same manner, a man following the reverse path turns to meanness and degradation through worldliness. The good thought power Vohuman that gives light to the eye (i.e. the understanding) of man is (obtained) by loving the powerful wealth (i.e. course of life), which makes for improvement. He who is without this wealth is without the above-mentioned things (for the improvement of wisdom.)

Men ought to raise themselves to illustrious positions by worldly knowledge and by education (which enables them) to read and write. They should keep themselves with the bounds of law and order by the precepts of the faith and purchase many books containing wise sayings.
For obtaining immortality (in the next world) they should duly praise the helping Yazad's and struggle with (the wicked.) Many virtuous men improve and exalt the one substance (i.e. the soul) by praising the Yazad's. (The arch-priests) explain to the people the nature of the several (wicked beings) who are always for quarrel, inimical to the creations of (Ohrmazda) and helpful to the creatures of darkness (Men) ought to acknowledge they are the giver of existence the Creator who endowed living men with bodies possessing complete supremacy with the help of fire and water.

Those who do not turn to the faith of the Daevas (i.e. those who cling to the religion of Mazda-worship with firm faith) must be rewarded. Those who lead mankind with the intention of making them recognize one God must be made the governors of the world, and those who keep to the mandates of religion must be called (men) of pure origin. In the same manner, the contemplators of Divine knowledge must be rewarded with such gifts, as they desire.

Things that were fit to be supplied at some place for (keeping up) the existence (of animated beings) must be most certainly borne there in any way (that is possible;). As for instance, the water of the river which gives strength to life, and medicine prepared in cold and warm water for (removing) discomfort from the soul (both in life and at the time of death.) It is the good thoughtful (physician) that knows the proper medicine for (giving) blood, shining (complexion), consciousness, and taste.

Just as the Flame is through live fire, light through flame, and twilight after light, in the same manner, the greater or less recovery (of animate beings) from many a disease, takes place by means of medicinal herbs.

Just as the date tree grows up from the date-stone, in the same manner the production of man is through the act of procreation.

For the connection of progeny (i.e. for

begetting offspring) the sexual congress of one person with another is (essential.)

Permanence of life depends on the soul's connection with the body.

Rain or the Yazad's bestowing rain is the cause of prosperity to living beings.

The permanence of friendship and amity is through seeing and conversing with one another.

How is existence brought about? Just as one substance is evolved out of another according to its own laws and in the finite time (fixed for it.)

What the produce of a certain city is, or what grows up in its lands is understood by knowledge of (the city.)

The first gift of life-giving Creator is as regards the soul. The students of the Manthras properly understand the different gifts relating to the soul, bestowed by the Creator. Nor are the proper remedies for the last pangs of the soul hidden from them.

Chapter 7

Questions from The Denkard

The following are the questions of those who retail scandal against honest religious beliefs.

Q. Is the potent being (God) finite or not?

A. The answer is this that the leader of religion (the chief arch-priest) remains glorious by receiving God's halo of exalted worth. In the same manner, he is the agent (of God) to encourage people to perform works of religion by means of his far-seeing understanding. Therefore, by actions unworthy of a leader he does not lose his previously obtained position as a leader of religion.

Q. Is the potent being (God) capable of wisdom to a limited extent or more the (i.e. is He omniscient or not?)

A. The star-readers (i.e. astrologers) understand the worth of the allotment (of destiny by the stars).

How long is the chief allotting (stars) to move in bad aspects? How long are they in conjunction with the malignant owner of bad aspects? How long does the man (influenced by such stars) work in the way of wisdom? The laws relating to these and other (astrological) details the astrologers learn from writings on the earth (i.e. from astrology). Astrologers can foretell the good events of a man's (life) from his horoscope. The physicians can explain the details (regarding the health of the body, the safety of the body and the connection of the soul with the body. Those who are connected (with a man) infer from his outward movements his life, the destruction of his life, his actions and his investigations. Knowledge of the substances and of the creation of time and place is (attained) by (the explanation of) the creator (i.e. by inspiration.) Through the nature (of the substance) is (attained) the knowledge of its qualities and through creation its existence (is known). Knowledge of perverse substances is attained through understanding the nature of acceptable substances.

Q. Does (God) irradiate His glory through intermediaries?

A. The obedient soul (created by) the Almighty is so because of the connection and radiance of the immortal (Yazad's) whose knowledge the holy God has bestowed (onto the obedient soul). With the blessing of that radiance, that (man) becomes famous by performing every earthly action according to his will and through unanimity with the opponent (Ganamino) man prevents his nature (from virtuous actions). He who completely reforms the different natures of the adversary's (connections) renders himself fortunate. His progeny keeps to the original (nature from which he is sprung). The race of horses is (sprung up) from the first horse; the production of orange is from the first orange tree. In the same manner, that a man should completely improve his progeny, for its safety and continuance, is necessary for making his race famous.

Through abiding by the mandates of God observing the precepts of religion on earth the soul of man and his progeny acquire an insight into the things relative to the good creation (i.e. the spiritual world), eternal wisdom and (eternal) time (as naturally as) the eye (acquires) the power of vision. By means of this, every nature keeps his material existence connected with God, in the same manner as twilight is connected with light.

The religious governor conversant with religion is a great instrument, for the worship and praise of God.

Firstly-- (The king) must be susceptible of

beneficent wisdom and useful to those related with him. Secondly -- The king is supposed to pay respect to worthy beings (i.e. men walking in the path of God). Thirdly-- (The king) is supposed to be without deviation from divine mandates, fulfilling God's wish, and is reckoned superior through (possessing) God's wisdom. Fourthly -- (The king) does not become supreme by disowning the superiority of the potent Yazad's, but is supposed to perform other dishonest actions, through adverse intentions. (The king) who deals justice, according to the precepts of God's revelation, has an effective remedy for the grief's of the people of this world and keeps his subjects well off by means of justice, that the (king) preserves his dignity with permanent fame by means of these (his) actions, (which are) without harm and bring on prosperity. It behooves the King to inflict on men two kinds of punishment for their offenses in order to establish his fame. The one (punishment) is bodily (i.e. giving physical labor to the body) and the other is the infliction of fine. The sage judges, studying the Manthras, know every kind of punishment. The man under the dominion of (the demons) the instructors of sins declares (in a court of justice) that he is a witness, and gives harmful evidence, in spite of not seeing (anything). How can that man receive salvation from the sin of unfaithfulness? The students of justice discern the (real) thoughts of these men of (wicked) connection, because of the lodgment of the Yazad's among them, (which lodgment is) like the lodgment of water in clay. The connection of adverse (i.e. unjust) judges is harmful (to the Yazad's); therefore, they are regarded as not connected (with the Yazad's). For this it reasons the substance under the dominion of the Yazad's is considered to be of exalted (i.e. supernal) existence, and the substance not under their dominion is called (the thing) of darkness (infernal) and non- existence. Again, the substance under the dominion of (Ganamino) the despoiler of existence enjoys the (wicked) existence of its master. The substance possessing the wisdom of the Yazad's acts in the creation, just like an effulgent supernal power. As long as the substance during its life does not excite (itself) (with Ahriman's power), it is said to be of proper connection. And, those men of whom Yazads are supposed to be the masters are the servants of God, enjoying His favor; harm cannot reach them.

Q. If the potent being (God) were infinite, how can He be called potent being? Again, how can one possessing finite power be called the potent being?

A. (In reply to the questions: Has God who is worthily of (eternal) existence any limit? and in knowledge is He capable to a certain extent or is His capability beyond limit?) The explanation therefore is that God has concern with finite time, and is Lord of finite knowledge, but He being (himself) without limit as to knowledge and time, is said to be of unlimited time and unlimited knowledge.

Q. Should all works be done at their proper (i.e. destined) time? Can they be done at other times? Can a work be without reward?

A. (Is there any transmission of Light from one to another? The answer to which is that) the God of Existence is the best leader (of the world temporal and spiritual) and He is capable of imparting His own Light to another.

Q. Are all works done at present in accord with know-ledge and wisdom? If a work is connected with the original strength, (i.e. has come from the source of goodness, God) how can it be said in light of the faith to belong to infinite time?

A. To the people who have existence God, through his chief creation through the good-thinking angelic power grivet a comprehension of the end of their creation.

Q. How can the leader of darkness be truthful?

Who leads the true leader astray?

A. Those that are dwellers in Hell have been mentioned as (inmates) of Darkness, not of Light. Whatever elements there are of heat, cold, moisture, and dryness in the bodies of those (i.e. men) living as the companions of the Yazads, they have been created (by God) for doing the work of the body. They thus serve to keep in good order the vitality and are the means of keeping the body sound.

In the same way (evil agencies) that do harm (to the body) cause the elements of cold and dryness to dwell in the body, and permeate the human system to the injury of the elements of the heat and moisture that do the work of vivifying the body. The coexistence of these four elements in equitable relations with each other tends to the amelioration of the body.

Q. How does the life-giver (God) give outward form (to all substances?)?

A. Unfair and defective agencies cause harm to the body. 'The Life-Giving One' (God) is not sustainer of the adverse creation. All men oppose, obstruct, and fight with one another for the existence of the principle with which they are connected (i.e. are either for Spenamino or

Ganamino). Nay, the different opponents who fully grace the principle to which they belong are related to their kind (i.e. to the side to which each has given his choice). Thus, a thing of cold (essence) is known to suppress beat, and a thing of dry (essence) to suppress moisture. When the representative of one side encounters the representative of the other, it is not for suppressing him altogether, but with the motive of obstructing, the work assigned to him by (natural) Law. The uniform state of the blood is due to the dryness, which is related, to heat and moisture, which is related to cold. In the same way an organic body is rendered unfit when heat accompanies moisture, and cold accompanies dryness; the blood stops in consequence, and at once flows in the opposite direction. As the sources of the elements bring about dryness connected with heat, and moisture connected with cold. There is much a commingling of heat with cold and of dryness with moisture, which this relation being kept up in the body, it conduces to the proper animation of the same, and the body always remains busy at its work along with the connected Yazads. All misunderstandings and quarrels, which now occur at times between individuals, are due to the related influences becoming unworthy. This is brought about by the lower existences (i.e. the evil powers of the demons) commingling in the body. When those of one kind make a sudden attempt to make the body unfit, it is brought into affinity with death. And the ruin of the body is through its being enfeebled in many ways by destructive evil tendencies. Also the Spirit that is opposed to the vital action of the body is the (invisible) one that tries to make the body act contrary to uniform laws. The man works for good life of his body through the spiritual powers, which work for his (virtuous) existence. The cessation of the work of existence, pertaining to the good recompense of the soul, is due to the body becoming lightless (i.e. lifeless), by the development of the work of the destructive forces (in the body) the enfeebling powers therein are strengthened. The good bright Yazads that have relation with men keep them from contact with the adverse forces (i.e. the demons). It is mentioned in the religious books that it is through the influence of the spiritually existing Yazads residing in men, that they (men) are free from various kinds of harm and evil.

Q. How can the faithful of this world perform actions the aim and object of which would be the same as (the aim and object) of (the Yazads and Amahraspands) the radiant being that always carry out God's wishes?

A. Again, among the various professions the choicest is that of the heads of the religion, and the one pertaining to the attainment of the love of the Yazads, and that of loading oneself to the performance of noble actions in this, world.

Q. In what ways is the worshipper of God distinct from the one who scorns Him? Why should one who has power of endurance complain (against pain?)? How can a substance become very famous?

A. The knowledge of what man's duties are and what they are not is acquired by man through there being a sufficient number of the family of the religious leaders (i.e. through there being a sufficient number of Dasturs and Mobeds informed in religion), who are the ardent (i.e. careful) preservers of the Avesta and its commentaries. They are thus the expounders of the religion in public to the people of the world, the instructors of the philosophy of the Religion to the people, and proclaim of the (religious) truth to those that argue perversely against it. They are those that embarrass all famine-producers and ravagers of fertility. They are those that attract people to the worship of God, and make them obey their kings and honor the decisions of their judges. They are those that make the people of the four divisions (the Athonrnan, the Artheshtar, the Vastriosh and the Hutokhsh) illustrious in their respective occupations.

In addition, by means have Questions and answers pertaining to Ohrmazda, they make them devoted to religion, students of religion, and worshippers of God. They keep in currency the requirements other the other Athonrnan, (i.e. they supply them the things they want), and fulfill their wishes, whereby good and respectable families are maintained honorably. Those (men) that are the instructors in the Zartosht [Zoroastrian] religion are the promoters of the desire for religion and the disseminators of the knowledge of it. The other thing pertaining to the Mazdayasnian faith, (i.e. wisdom), which, in so far as it serves the purpose of clearing up all misunderstanding (i.e. doubts), is pleasing to those that tread the path of God, is to be kept pure. And the new seekers after knowledge must, by being put in the way of acquiring it, are kept above want. In him that does not advance his community, and forbids not men from immoral acts, good faith should not be placed. Then he should never be regarded as a leader (of the community) or as one who can remove the apprehensions of each individual, or as one who can make the other creation (i.e. the atheists) obedient to God.

Through repentance of sin is attainable the receiving go the recompense for righteousness and the discarding of sin. And after that there is no occasion for punishment. Connection with the med for a single act of righteousness is the cause of the reduction of the punishment for the sins (of that man). It is God's object to make those, who disobey the commands of the king, deserving of various kinds of punishments by way of justice. Among them, the one who disobeys the commands (of the king), and the one who is imprisoned for all the offenses relating to the soul, are to be released by order of the State. In addition, if a prisoner has been put in imprisonment by recourse to ways contrary to orders, (i.e. in contravention of the laws of justice), for causing grievous wrong to the soul, it is a kind of oppression. Again, at the bidding of the physician that heals the disorders of the soul (i.e. the Dasturs of the religion), it would be conformable to religion to let off a highwayman from capital punishment.

Q. The Sun shines on the earth according to the time of the season, Why are (then) some places without the heat of the illuminator? Although (substances) improve by means of the illuminating Sun, some places are (even) at noontide moist and dirty. Why should it be that one place is moist in spite of the noonday heat whereas another gets more than its portion of the light of the Sun?

Q. How is the inability to look at the effulgent

light (of the Sun to be explained?)? Why is the weakening and enfeebling of the eyesight thereby? How can pain proceed from the luminous Sun, which derives its power from God?

A. For the leaders of the world -- those that are crowned with supreme majesty (i.e. the king and the Dasturs) -- the equitable Government of iranshehr is feasible through illustrious judges -- the dispensers of justice. The maintenance of the sovereignty over the seven regions by the Zoroastrians is due to there being an abode within them of Religion, the Kayanian majesty, and other glories. Again, the means that they have for living in exuberance (i.e. in comfort), and the cause of all their pristine greatness and supremacy are due to their having within them the coming and going of the Yazads (i.e. to their intercourse with the Yazads and Amahraspands). It is because of this very sovereignty (endowed with Yazads majesty) that such a king of Iran is able to invest with power the rulers of the seven regions. As the flame of a fire is due to its relation with the inward glow, and as light is due to its relation with the flame, in the same manner is Wisdom due to Religion, and superior power is attainable (by man) by his relation with the instructor of the Religion. And through an insight into (i.e. comprehension of) it is the (righteous) existence of man, and through his connection with the open path (of religion) is the test (of man). Then through such power (of religious wisdom) is the body able to perform the functions necessary to the soul. And through soundness of the body is the preservation of the soul. All Iranians (i.e. Mazdayasnian) by so regulating themselves can live with a superior kind of strength. Those of the citizens that give instruction in (the acquirement of) knowledge, spiritual forces, art, courage, physical strength, and prosperity, make the rule of the king of Iran supreme, auspicious, and honored.

The greatness of the Iranians (i.e. the Mazdayasnian) is owing to truthfulness in all matters, kind regard, and meditation on the design of Providence in all-powerful creations. By these means, they keep in affinity to their source (i.e. their Creator), and obtain victory over men of the opposite nature and over the ignoble and wild-looking subject nations of other cities. Again, the Mazdayasnian should give good advice to the people that are of harsh and abominable traits, evil-worshippers, and enfeebled, so that these may not waste their life in vain actions. As they should form men, who are not of good essence (i.e. are evil), into being good men, like the present good-thinking pious men, who are particularly careful in their adherence to noble speech and in keeping aloof from base things.

Had not the people of the good Creation put themselves at first into an awkward position before the rulers, by the use of (inept) expressions, they would never have become, but could have remained with their faculties on alert. In addition, had they not in this way come to disregard the divine commands, and to deprive themselves of the intellect guarded over by the Yazads, they would have been able to understand what things are to be done and what not to be done. And they would have known that the Yazads effulgence of the luminous soul couldn't for long dwell in the body just as the sun refrains from making luminous (for all time) the good things that shine by the sun's light. (The Yazads radiance) it has been known to interrupt by the man's being very careless. Therefore it is that for certain reasons contradictory words should not be uttered in the presence of rulers; and in order to keep oneself in good repute one should, in their presence, give expression to one's THOUGHS after mature consideration.

Premeditation is necessary in questioning and in answering, and then the question may be put, or the reply given, in the proper way. It is the way of the priests of the false religions not to act with good sense, before they are overpowered.

Q. Do the Yazad's guarding the earth give up the work of man's salvation through fear of the wicked one?

A. Before putting a question in one's turn, one should catch the drift of the opponent's argument. Again, in a discussion, he that speaks much should not be checked, but his reasoning should be well listened to. Also, in a discussion, if there be a question, it should be satisfactorily answered. If there be many such questions they should be dealt with in various ways.

The perfect glory (i.e. the Divine gift) that fits men for leadership is of the nature, viz. that such people take upon themselves to answer properly the questions of those that argue well; but he that has faculty for (mere) fault such a disputant does not argue for self-improvement. Nor is his discussion pertaining to the soul, and therefore such discussion should be dropped. The discussion which is beneficial, and pertaining to the salvation (of the soul) from Hell, and for the welfare of the soul, should not be set aside, but should be carried out to the solution. Nor should one refrain from exposing falsehood, wrong ideas, and wickedness. To secure their deliverance from Hell, they (the people) should be led, by all kinds of truth, to have implicit and unshaken faith; and from this there should be no turning aside for whatsoever reason. And like the spring season one should show himself at his best in his ardor (for expounding the religion). If the signification of anything (pertaining to religion) were not clear, it should be given out as unintelligible. In addition, in the argument whatever is worth esteeming should be appreciated in detail Moreover, no wrong deed that might have been done should be admired. Nevertheless, the right action only that has been per-formed by the help of God should be accepted as beneficial.

The foremost leader of the religion (i.e. the Dasturan Dastur [Zarathushtrotema]) should imbue the people with ardor for the religion, and induce them to be very industrious, in order to make them excel in their routine of work, and should exhort them to acquire other noble arts.

Those that have been in touch with the Yazads (viz. the believing Mazdayasnian), should, by girding themselves for the fight, making use of the right understanding (about Spenamino and Ganamino), ward off one of them (the Ganamino), and follow the other (the Spenamino). And with the strength and courage derived from the Spenamino they should attack the other (Ganamino), and (by the help of the Spenamino) they should obtain the nourishment of their nature. Until the end, the fight should be maintained with Ganamino, who should never be regarded as having received good training.

Q. How can the expelled Blemish-giver be (present) in him who is innocent? If God should recompense them and make them, of great worth how can the truthful ever think of sorrow and the charitable bestowals of corn [i.e. grain] ever suffer from hunger?

A. The charitable man is he who bestows in charity from his own (acquired) wealth. In addition, the truthful man is he who never speaks untruth on behalf of or about another person.

The grateful man is he who recognizes an obligation. Gratitude should be shown towards him to whom one, like a dependent, is under obligation for his life. Moreover, secondly, gratitude should be shown towards him who having the power to harm hath done no harm; and finally, when one has experienced all possible good from him, one must assuredly show one's gratitude by words and deeds.

Those that are engaged in the inquiry (i.e. search) after immortality, acceptable to God, and (are the friends) of the benevolent (i.e. the imparters of religious instruction), of other benefactors, are the procurers of other felicities for their kith and kin; and by not bearing any ill-feeling towards robbers and other harm-doers, towards prisoners, and other criminals and wretched people. And by making them happy and faithful, they prove themselves possessors of the good strength worth being grateful for (i.e. Those who showing compassion towards robbers, prisoners, and sinners, lead them to improvement, really bring them under their obligation by making them staunch believers (in the faith). However, by cherishing hatred towards them they are held to be in danger of becoming guilty.

A father ought to reform his son, if he were unworthily, by inculcating in him noble thoughts (i.e. by religious instruction). Therefore, if a man from want of assistance were incapable of doing any work, he should, in order, that he may surmount all kinds of wretchedness, be given the means to acquire more wealth.

Q. People consider the evidence of (persons) of high descent as throwing more light than that, of untrue speakers; but why should they be considered of high descent and lofty dignity if they serve the will of sovereigns of low worth. One whom God has declared to be of (royal) family in the Avesta is not to be considered royal but if (such a person) serve not the will of wicked sovereigns should his royal descent be acknowledged.

A. A discussion on religion may be entered into with those of the controversialists on religious subjects, who are so (learned) as to be able to give authoritative decision on all subjects. Thus the truth on their side being known, they may have no occasion on punish, according to the dictates of the Nasks (of the Avesta), the priests of the false religion.

A certain nation's scriptures, known by the name of True [Torah] (i.e. the scriptures of the Jews viz. the Torat or the Injil) have been regarded as the words of the devils, and are not worthy of belief. Nothing mentioned therein deserves to be done for the benefit of the creation. Because the writing makes mention of the irrelevant matters which ought not to have been introduced therein. Whatever therein is not good writing is the concoction of various writers, therefore such writings is said to be of the soul-cramping tendency, and those concocted accounts the Jews regards the revelation of the original creation (i.e. pertaining to the celestial Yazads).

To the Rummies who help the Yazdan-worshippers of good wisdom (i.e. who help those of the Mazdayasnian faith) and to others who live a similar (good) life, should be expounded the original text of the 'Ganj-i-Shaspigan.' (In other words, the Jews and the Greeks who wish to believe in the Mazdayasnian religion), and such of them as have no faith in their own, and want to improve, should be thoroughly instructed in the religion.

If in other countries there be any writings (respecting our religion) worth reading, new, ameliorating, good, and divinely inspired, these should be procured; and there should be no backwardness in the study of them and in the researches into them. And whatever in the writings of other nations is unbelievable should not be accepted.

The nature that has concern with the greatest development of wisdom (i.e. is studious) must be admired. Attention should be given to the writings of (the men of) other countries and the same should not be destroyed.

In these writings (of men of other countries) if there be any passages and aphorisms pertaining to the service of the one God. It is not every comment thereon or every maxim that is to be indiscriminately given publicity out of the body of those writings and maxims; but we should make from them a selection of the original (sacred) passages and maxims (pertaining to our religion). The books in the Ganj-i-Shaspigan should be read with careful attention to all the passages.

In these writings, (i.e. those pertaining to our religion) the human body is treated of in four parts, of which the head, 'is said to be presided' over by the Athornan (i.e. the priestly) class. With the hand by the Artheshtar (i.e. the warrior) class, the stomach by the agricultural class, along with the leg by the people who follow good avocations for livelihood.

The human soul is said to have the chief control over all the above-mentioned four classes, and the soul itself is said to be under the dominion of God.

A twofold object evidently influences the words and deeds of every man. His first object is to qualify himself for the final (welfare), and his second object is to endow himself with noble thoughts by so training himself for the profession (of piety.)

The Iranians (i.e. the God-fearing Mazdayasnians) are deserving of praise because of all their honest dealings, while dishonest and blemish men deserve to be condemned.

The celebrated erudite Seneca's of Rum and the servants of India have shown an appreciation of and have much admired the foresighted persons of Iran. They adopted their expressions and ideas, and on seeing, the great worth of these wise men of Iran showed their preference for them.

Q. How can the Emperor Ardashir Papakan's sovereignty be acknowledged in spite of the severance of authority from several of his direct ancestors?

For the same reason many scholars became worthy to obtain high position and favor from the (Iranian) rulers. And by obtaining high recompense and support (from the Iranian leaders), they in order to get a full reward of their merit, much dreaded these leaders in this world, and were much afraid of punishment in the next. Moreover, they abstained from these blemishes, so that they might continue (to receive) honest recompense from their Iranian superiors who could hold them back (from such blemishes.)And they themselves, (i.e. the leaders), in their desire to obtain a good recompense for their souls, abstained from any carelessness that might cause them to be miserable in the abode or palace, village or city of the next world; arid they never gave way to any lustful passion. Nevertheless, they cherished the learned men, with the view of securing distinction as men of worth. And they were held in high esteem among the rulers; for from the illiterate is not to be expected the approval of a noble action, or mature consideration; nay, on the contrary, there proceed from them various evils. The unwise have not the tact to acquire the desirable sufficient independence pleasing to the rulers. Therefore, an honored ruler, by keeping aloof from the unwise, can put himself in the way of acquiring the desired degree of excellence. His endeavors should not be directed towards any base or injurious ends, but he should strive by counteracting such tendencies to attain to a high position in the next world. Such a ruler gives good attention to the orders he issues and to other regulations (pertaining to the state); and thereby ensures a pleasant enjoyment of his dignity.

The (State-administering) chiefs should choose as their king a person of high rank and good repute. None but a man of worth should be elected king. For this purpose, a distinguished person related to the chiefs should be secured. Individual predilections should have no weight in the choice of a king. Further, if the person (fixed upon) is not of kingly descent, another one should be procured from a different place, as in the interests of justice the election (of a king) is indispensable.

To those wise men who choose to retire from the post conferred on them by the king, or who, in order that they may live in contentment, give up the business or service, which was entrusted to them, -- to those, that entertain such good notions of securing happiness, no benefit can accrue in life by this relinquishment (of their work). Because, if against their wishes they be again forcibly carried off by order of the State, and be forced to resume their work, they would find no enjoyment in it. Therefore they should stick to and perform faithfully whatever works appears to them to be of public or private benefit.

The learned kings of the State, with the view of ruling with a high degree of efficiency, should strive (for the fulfillment), by Divine Grace, of new and noble aspirations, such as: -- encouraging the learned, the illustrious, and the charitable, being grateful towards those who are loyal to and have affection for the State. Conferring of bounty on the suppliants and on those that are in solicitude owing to poverty, gratifying with a good and befitting remuneration annually, the learned men who may be in constant anxiety for having to labor for their food and livelihood, along with the giving of everyday donations, according to the needs of their circumstances. For the glorification of the (next) spiritual world to the conspicuous true believers who come into the (royal) presence, on those that arte misers greedy for amassing worldly pelf, on those that have no reverence for the soul. In addition, on those that abstain not from sins, nothing should be bestowed, so that they might not get facilities for taking to drink and of robbing the wise of their due.

Before putting a question in one's turn, one should catch the drift of the opponent's argument. Again, in a discussion, he that speaks much should not be checked, but his reasoning should be well listened to. Also, in a discussion, if there be a question, it should be satisfactorily answered. If there be many such questions they should be dealt with in various ways.

Every man that has a material body should regard his own marriage as a good work incumbent on him to perform. He should strive diligently at his avocation that he may live in happiness. He should take good care of the materials of power (i.e. good deeds for the next world) that his lifetime may pass in contentment. Moreover, he should promote the marriages of others.

If thou wish to be educated, give thy choice to the works of the foresighted (i.e. works pertaining to God). If thou wouldst avoid hard times, refrain from giving thy approval to works involving afflictions of various kinds.

Who are our instructors? The Dasturs learned in religion.

In what subjects have they to instruct us? In noble things (belonging to) three (places.)

Of all noble things and places this world the next world and the transposing (i.e. the final imperishable embodiment).

Of what thing should we choose the good recompense? Of rightness.

How can we get instructions on this subject? From the Dastur of the religion says.

On our soul's parting from the body that will take us (to the spiritual world), and by what path, the good contriving quest (i.e. the guardian angel of the good conscience) by way (of Heaven), (Space the Universes around all things).

By what powers can we attain to the lodgment

(within us) of good THOUGHTS? By the resolve of obedience of God, how can we acquire the resolve of such obedience?

By concentrated meditation through the acuteness of the intellect, I, for once, teach you two words of wisdom -- That you should do good deeds, and should refrain from doing deeds, which should not be done.

What deeds should we eschew and what deeds should we do? Evil THOUGHTS, evil words, and evil deeds we should eschew; and good THOUGHTS, good words, and good deeds we should adopt. Each of these maxims is good for you.

Chapter 8

AHRIMAN THE DESTROYER

Ahriman has been known, by several names, since 2,500 BCE, and was also created to bring fear to all civilizations.

It is said that Ahriman appears approximately every 1000 years, and destroys or takes over the Earth, bringing Darkness for a time. Although it has been interpreted many ways throughout the ages, it is curious that he has not made an appearance in the last 4000 years. In fact, no one, Evil Being has arrived to destroy the Earth.

Interpreted many ways through the ages, it is said that Ahriman comes around, every One Thousand years, to destroy or to take over the Earth, and bringing Darkness to the Earth for unknown length.

Humans actually “create” these Evil Beings simply by thought, and Ahriman is a manifestation of this thought due to mankind's fear of evil. In a previous book, I pointed out that people do not realize the Forces and magnitude of energy and thought. Humans invent the evil beings by simple thought, and likewise, the good.

What follows on these next few pages are some ideas of what these Beings look like based upon the thoughts that people have conjured. These pictures of the beings are the same from generation to generation, and yet, neither they nor the stories do not change.

Many of these names are quite familiar to you, and are interchangeable. Names from our mythologies, legends, and most from a religious aspect, exist even today. Names such as:

Kronos (Cronos)
Seth
Mephistopheles
Saturn
Ahriman
Lucifer

At the end of every age, these Dark beings are associated with Famine, Destruction, and other upheavals. There are many stories of these Beings that have been associated with all these changes. While these are nothing more than a cycle of the Earth, people need to assign them to some being whether real or imagined.

One of these stories:

When the Jews reached Canaan they changed from nomads to a settled and agricultural people without a precedent for agriculture or settling down. However, it was inevitable that many of the Canaanites' habits, customs, and attitudes should be integrated with the Hebrew people. The inhabitants of Canaan had a system of worship that paralleled that of Zarathustra. They worshiped Baal and the female counterparts, Baal's, the most famous of which was Asteroid (Ishtar, Astarte).

While the Jews also worshiped the same, over time they converted the gods of the Canaanites into their own devils just as followers of Zarathustra incorporated their own ideas from India, creating their own pantheon along with the devils of their neighbors Nevertheless, it took some time to abolish the autochthonous deities that existed in Palestine, especially since many of the Jews worshipped them. Thus, read in Ezekiel that Jerusalem was hotbed of pagans.

Under Samuel, Saul, David, and Solomon, and war after war, Israel was finally unified into a nation (Circa 1040, BCE). After the death of Solomon, who began the building of the Temple at Jerusalem in 969, another division of Israel occurred, and split the kingdom into Judah and Israel. This was the period of the pre-exilic prophets who gave statement to the fascinosum and tremendous aspects of the monotheistic deity Jehovah, or Elohim, a word that originally meant gods in the plural.

Question: So, who flourished in the 8th century B.C.E.?

Answer: Beings of half human and half animal that people generalize as evil / negative. But, they are very wrong in that realization. I hinted at these beings in book one, but did not elaborate. Some of these beings came into existence through the interaction of humans and animals. These interactions were mainly due to the energy of Terra, or Earth. Earth flipped on its axis during the second Age of Atlantis sometime around 56,000 BCE. The guardians were charged with teaching them to understand their existence. Upon their deaths, it was also their task to help separate these two Beings souls, which were merged together in one body.

Simultaneously, Atlantean scientists were conducting genetic experiments creating the same beings artificially effectively replacing nature. But, they were far more destructive and rebellious than nature's creations. They had no knowledge why they existed, and sewed havoc and destruction among civilizations. And, this is why humans considered them evil and/or devils.

The stories that were created, were of

negativity and evil. Mainly, because these beings left Atlantis and went to other continents. Which those inhabitants, of those other continents knew nothing about these beings. Since, these inhabitants were witnessing, this destructiveness and chaotic events from these beings. In addition, those stories are still told today without the understanding about these beings and how they came to be.

These Beings are not evil by any means. Yes. They are different due to the type of energy that the Earth was entering at that time.

I urge all to learn and understand the truth about all these beings that existed during the old ancient Ages of Terra.

This is the only way all will truly understand about the life that once existed, and the life that will become part of Terra again. It will also help you to understand the energy of the evolution process of life.

One thing is for sure you will not learn the Truth of the ancient Ages, through your religions. They know about all of this. Nevertheless, they are the ones that are creating this fear towards these beings. Therefore, the only way that is left for you to learn the truth is to go out and research it on your own.

There are many stories, which are told about these ancient Beings that existed eons ago, and they are all true. The early stories are of negative, but if you keep on digging deeper into these stories, you will see that, these stories will change from negative towards the positive. Then you will see for yourself on how these stories came to be changed. Which were to create fear towards these other beings?

It is up to us, the guardians to teach everyone the truth on how these stories of the old ancient ages, were twisted and turned inside out. Which was to bring about fear and confusion about all these Beings that are in existence? Just, because these beings are different, does not make them evil / negative, at all.

The task of these guardians were to, untwist, and teach the truth about the existence of life, of who you all are, (the human race) and to help you to understand about these other Beings, which are among you today.

Remember, all beings have a role to fulfill that exists. If it to be, within the plane that we exists on or if it is below or above us. This also goes for the Beings that are moving from Spirit to First dimension and First to Second dimensions. Then the Second to the Third dimension and as the people of Earth is moving from Third to the Fourth and Fifth dimensions.

You, also have those Beings going from Fourth and Fifth dimensions, moving to the Sixth dimension, and so on.

These Beings are not what you and the

religions are making them out to be. Yes, these types of beings do exist, like many other beings that you are not aware of at this time.

The only Dark and upheaval times, that we are all, witnessing on Terra (Earth) is - our own Thoughts, which is being brought about by, The religions and the governments of this world.

The typical ideas of the religious Devils

A Zoroastrian demon being, that is to come around, once every 1,000 years for the battle of Light and Dark. So, they say....

She is called, 'Lilith', she is also known as Adams first wife as you have learned earlier. It is said that she 'is also known to be seen with Baal and Samael after leaving Adam over 170,000 years ago.

Today, there are humans controlling each other through the use of fear in the guise of Churches and Religions as well as governments, who use weapons that they have created in order to control everyone around the world. With wars all over the world, these humans create them, then blame it on others while they absolve themselves. And, religions use the wars to tell their congregations that these events are the "end times".

The alien beings portrayed gods and demons giving their all to hide their true identities, while creating false belief systems under the veils of Darkness. Humans' Spiritual growth of the Universal Knowledge was denied to them, and strayed from the true meaning of knowledge that was being sent by the Benevolent Ones, which were not gods or devils that never existed in any universe, but are, instead, higher evolved Beings!

During their reigns, and with every chance

that the people tried to learn the truth, these deities lied to divert the people from the real truth. While the Benevolent Beings strived to teach the inhabitants about the truth, those deities twisted that knowledge to hide it. These deities had gained those peoples believes in them and no other beings. Humans wanted to learn, but the deities continue to insist that the supernatural was forbidden – taboo. Urging the humans to stay clear of the Benevolent Beings became their focus, repeating this over and over until the people believed. It is a fact that telling someone the same thing over and over, again, eventually becomes truth, and humans are easily susceptible to repetition.

Battles with all Races

The second epoch of wars was fought with the Lower Beings vs. The Benevolent Ones. Several battles have taken place within the last seven thousand years. The following explains:

- Seven Thousand years ago: The wars of the Lower Beings and the Benevolent Ones, or Dark vs. Light, were waged against one another for our sector of the Universe. The one who survived would reign over this

Universe. The forces of Light stepped back, and allowed the forces for Dark create (chaos) havoc. While the Dark were distracted by creating chaos, the Light put aside their teachings, and placed the emphasis on their secret battle against the Dark forces.

- Five Thousand years ago: The Tower of Babel. Whereas The Benevolent Beings would not have kept the people from learning the truth, the so-called gods and devils began to punish the people for trying to learn of the universal laws and the truth of Spiritual Awakening.

- Simultaneously with the Tower of Babel, the Benevolent Ones brought forth "the "Ark of the Covenant"", which was to aid in the battle of Light and Dark. The "Ark of the Covenant" was an off-world device that amplified the energy of Light to spill over into the Dark, and through the veil of illusion. In this way, the people would be given the chance to learn the Universal Truths.

- Four thousand years ago: The wars between the lower entities and Mankind prevailed.

2140 years ago: The epoch of Man against Man as well as religions against religions. Still, to this current time, we are still under the veil of illusions, which are being controlled by the lower entities. The Battle of Light and Dark are still being fought out in secrecy. But, as more and more people discover the Universal Truth, the realization that lies have controlled what we have been told is opening our eyes. By keeping us from our own right to grow and to awaken to the full Spiritual understanding of evolution, the Dark that has consumed humans is dissolving into the Light.

Chapter 9

Confusion

Through both recitation as well as the written word; from generation to generation over three to four thousand years, stories were told and retold of battles in ancient times. This resulted into "The One", or the Supreme Being that we know today, who created all with a "thought", which includes beings of all forms, both positive and negative, which are seen and unseen along with matter and antimatter, and many other forms.

As I mentioned earlier, thought, can be used to control and to destroy, and yet, it can be used as well to create at the same time. But, could one being's thought create life while another can use thought to control that being? And, if so, how can it be done?

...In the Beginning...

Was there a "beginning", or does a "beginning" just "appear" from the specific perspective of one's own life?

Well, there is never a Beginning it just appears to look like a Beginning from one's on POV. Perspective" "A view point of one's own life on where they were brought into existence" This is a never ending circle of life. To the mind of a human, "The One" was created in the front of their eyes – the one we call "God", today. As time goes on, thought is being "recycled" into creating to destroying to creating once again.

The beings of the past, whose thoughts created all in the past, are now experiencing their own worst nightmares! They are unaware that they are, now, experiencing their own thoughts. This includes the good of creation as well as the evil of destruction. Thus, they had created a "god, thought, and even being. Some people alive today are realizing that it was *they created all of these experiences* – taking everyone else along with them, while still others believe another "god" or "devil" is creating these experiences.

Today, these are perpetuating a thought of the End Times in a final battle. Nevertheless, they also sew fear of these Beings and the experiences in order to deviate our own train of thought toward a new "thought". These people have more to fear by these two beings, than of the thoughts of all other beings which exist.

Around 7,000 BCE, positive and negative energies have always been in existence from age to age until today's world. This current age, however, is the one that all Beings fear more than any other, because we consider this the "End Times". Many things which have been predicted really do seem to be taking place as I write this book.

Unfortunately, it is all built upon humans from the past who created these so-called Beings in order to represent the thoughts of positive and negative aspects of all their own thoughts. By doing so, it led to an influx of a great many manufactured beings which represent good and evil. People do not want to be held accountable for anything, so they seek to find others with which to blame. However, when there are no other people to blame, humans make up other beings whether real, or not, past or present, on whom to place that blame.

Regardless, the fact is that human created these beings, and it is time that humans begin to accept their responsibility for the creation of all Beings of good and evil. When things are good, they say that "this Being of wonderful power brought them as prophesized". Likewise, when things are good, they say that "this Being of evil brought these events as prophesized". It is this that was passed down from generation to generation. Today's humans do not realize this, therefore, they adopt the creations of mankind as their own without questioning it. Therefore, we continue the propagation of the past mistakes, and pass them on to our children, our children's children, who will believe exactly as we do; exactly as humans of the past who created it all.

Even despite the past creations, we still create faces of good and evil, light and dark, god(s) and devil(s), which are nothing more than only the positive and negative aspects of human creation.

A real example of this is through The Tower of Babel in Babylon. Humans attempted to rise up a Shem. **(Shem and the term shamain (heaven), stem from the root word shamah, meaning, that which is high ward).**

The Biblical tale of the Tower of Babel details the repopulating of Earth after the Deluge.

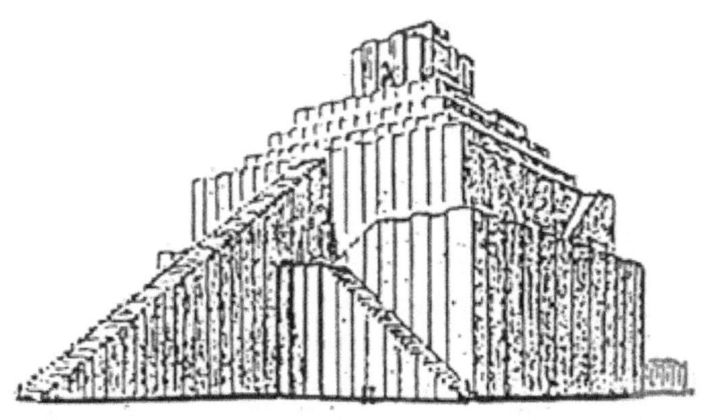

"Let us build us a city,
And a tower whose top shall reach the heaven;
And let us make us a Shem,
Lest we be scattered upon the face of the Terra,"

But this human scheme was not to God's liking. Therefore, the Lord came down, to see the city and the Tower, which the Children of Adam had erected. The Children of Adam are the Human Race.

And he said: "Behold,
All are as one people with one language,
And this just the beginning of their understandings;
Now, anything, which they shall scheme to do
Shall no longer be impossible for them."

And the Lord said to some of his colleagues...

"Come, let us go down,
And there confound their language so that they may
Not understand each other's speech,"
And the lord scattered them from there
Upon the face of the whole earth,
And they ceased to build the City.
Therefore was its name called Babel?
For there did the lord mingle the Terra's tongue."?

As long as humans could communicate in a single language, their abilities could continue to grow, and they could reach our evolution quickly. This was something that they had to prevent. So, confusion of languages was the solution. However, given time and thousands of years, many humans have learned other languages. Unfortunately, the majority of the world still must depend upon these people for translations. Even today, while the barriers of language did not last long, there are some things that just cannot be translated. Use of pictures and binary codes of computers are the easiest way to communicate one's meaning.

A different context concerning the Tower of Babel

Let's substitute the translate the word “shem” into "sky borne vehicle", rather than “Tower” for the word shem, which is used in the original Hebrew text of the Bible.

This changes the story completely. Now, the concern of mankind would become different. Mankind would be quite familiar with flying vehicles from the so-called “gods”. And, as humans spread to all points on Terra, they would lose contact with one another. So, in order to keep that from happening, they decided to build their own "sky borne vehicle(s) similar to their “gods”, and erect a tower to launch such vehicles. Even today, we have created these kinds of flying vehicles such as air ships, and of course, our planes, jets, and now, even spaceships that have carried humans to the moon. If those of the past had been allowed to continue to build ships for the sky, then where would we be today? Perhaps we would have taken to the stars for colonizations of humans, at the very least, within our own Milky Way Galaxy. What would we have discovered, by now? Stargates? Wormholes? The other side of Black Holes? The list is endless.

In the story of the "Epic of Creation" relates that the first "Gateway of the gods" was constructed in Babylon by the "gods", and these were called the Annunaki.

Today, however, instead of the "gods" coming to Earth to suppress humans from learning about the Knowledge of Life, this suppression has become the task of governments. Certain governments are, now, actually beginning to punish those of faith in many ways, demanding that humans follow the government, while religious groups demand that they follow them. In some cases, religions are the government, and vice versa.

The 'Ark of the Covenant' is, now, considered a weapon. That being said, only certain "priests" of God were allowed to carry the Ark. There is a bit of truth in this, because in the past, when these priests carried the Ark into a city, it activated the Ark's energy. Energy bolts came from it similar to lightning, which burst from the Ark itself, striking humans and killing them. After this event was finished, the priests would deactivate the ark, leaving the inhabitants of the city dead. Many Biblical cities discovered in recent years by archaeological digs, are found to have been burned, and left in rubble. But, there is even more proof of this. Pictographs, and drawings of the Ark of the Covenant, clearly show it being carried by priests, and lightning killing people leaving them laying on the ground. Some, then, proclaim that this is wrath of God. But, why would God want to kill people? The priests perpetuated the idea that the Ark only killed the wicked, and that God killed them to set an example for what would happen if they disobeyed God. It was, indeed, a punishment for their "wicked ways".

But, again, why would this god kill people, or destroy civilizations throughout history? What would be the reasoning? The answer is to keep the humans from becoming spiritually attuned and keep them knowing the truth about the true origins of human life. By destroying the advanced civilizations from time to time, this keeps them from understanding. And, it's always just as a civilization is growing to the point of almost discovery. Much like our time. Are we on the verge of destruction once again?

Guardians are on Earth as well as many other planets as well. They wish to teach all life about their Spiritual Evolution despite what these so-called gods desire, and The story about the Ark of The Covenant is the perfect example.

This is an excellent story about a time when the "gods" were angry with the human race who wanted to learn of the Knowledge of Life. It also shows how far the "gods" would go just to protect this knowledge. Not only would they destroy all life, but they would even destroy a planet(s) as well. The longer, and more aggressive humans try to learn of the truth, the more they are in danger of their own destruction by “gods”.

The Many Books of “gods”

Restating from earlier...most all ancient stories were either in recitation, or written. Because of the floods, earthquakes, volcanic activity, and other natural disasters, man is continually being forced to begin over. When these happen, most everything is destroyed – even up to those who keep oral stories, and any written stories. Humans are not really concerned with the keeping of the past in their struggles to just survive these disasters. The past knowledge takes a back seat to survival. And, it could last for hundreds of years, and generations, before the past becomes important once again.

6,000 years ago, books were written about life based upon God's words. Much of it is about how to live life. And, they took the word of these books without question, or even seeing the one who wrote the words. People began to record these stories to convince humans that if they did not follow the words, they would be punished. Many different versions were written, but have the same ending – obey or be punished. 3,500 years ago, those books of past, ancient civilizations were almost all wiped from the face of the Earth. And, those books that was not destroyed? They were placed in hiding by a few to preserve those stories about those lost ancient civilizations. These took it upon themselves to order new books from those earlier stories, and were called "Bible" in whatever form, then they were distributed around the world to the cultures and civilizations of that time. And, instead of inserting the rest of the story, these people decided that only they were worthy of knowing all of the truth, but that the other people in the world did not deserve the right to know. The past – our past – was effectively denied to humans, and created a great deal of confusion due to the inconsistency of these books. Most people don't even read these books, but depend upon someone else to tell them what they actually mean. And, all because they are confused about the content of these books, which only sounds like double talk to them. And, no wonder! This was deliberate! The truth has been altered, revised, rewritten, leaving out the truth. There are even some places, and everyone knows them, where the left out portions of these books have been hidden from mankind – deliberately. And, those who keep them hidden do so, because they believe they are the only ones who should know the truth. In consequence, they are the ones who rewrote mankind's story in a distorted, but bridged form of history. It was they who wanted to really “rule” the rest of us – to tell us what to do, and create fear of these “gods”.

These same religious “caretakers” do not tell their congregations to read for themselves, but the people have been “trained” not to read them, but to trust only them. But, even then, if we read it for ourselves, truth escapes us and are only fragments of a larger story. Those who do read it in its entirety are still missing parts of that story. The following stories of which we are all familiar are only written in part.

- The End Times
- Armageddon
- The Wraths of GOD
- The Rapture
- The Battle of Light and Dark
- GOD’s Destruction of The Earth
- Purgatory and Hell
- Heaven

Even while gruesome images of the final battle between good and evil are written, we till lack the whole story and the truth of our existence.

Even while gruesome images of the final battle between good and evil are written, we still lack the whole story and the truth of our existence.

At times, we stumble upon a cave or temple with drawings of gods and devils – some of half-animal and half-man. Yet, they are described as benevolent. If these beings did not exist, then why draw them?

During the reigns of these deities, they kept the people from learning about their true essence, of who they really are as beings. Kept them from learning the truth by With every chance that the people tried to learn of the Truth these deities kept the people from learning the truth by diverting them from the real truth – even if it meant making up lies. Thus, the people were deterred from following others who would impart the truth.

These Benevolent Beings tried to explain the truth to the people, but these other entities kept altering the knowledge while making that knowledge appear to be the wrong path. The lower beings fed upon the fear from the people.

Chapter 10

The Final Battle of Armageddon

What is The Final Battle; will it really be a final battle; or will it bring about destruction simply by thought? It is said that there is to be an end of the age when there will be a confrontation between good and evil upon the Earth…

While some may not want to accept this section others some of you will, look into this to compare it to what you find. In addition, the other part of you, will be familiar with, that this is true will do research and compare both. Many will recognize what is written, and know that we need to change things, now, as opposed to later.

Speaking to many people in researching, I discovered that most people believe in religion, and that they try to live as their "Bible" is written.

For centuries, prophetic messengers on Earth have spoken of the ultimate climactic battle between good and evil. The prophetic writer, John, in Satan's War Book, also known as the "Holy Bible," writes about the final battle at the end of the age, detailing it within the Book of Revelation – the time when the forces of good and evil clash, calling it the "Battle of Armageddon" (Rev16:16)

Biblical scholars reveal both a mystery and a lie concerning the Battle of Armageddon. Some claim that this great battle will be a physical battle with thousands upon thousands of horses and men, joining in hand-to-hand combat. The combatants in will be the God, Jehovah, with his forces are His "chosen people", the Jews. In other religions, such as Christianity, Jesus (Christ) will be His "chosen people". Other books throughout the world also detail this same battle which will be against the unbelievers and the forces of darkness. Jews call them the infidels, or gentiles, and are commonly called "goyium", meaning "cattle." Evil, of course, will be defeated, and the God Jehovah will triumph. Afterward, the "chosen people" will claim and occupy their "promised land", which is the Biblical land known as Palestine. From the "New Jerusalem", Jehovah will rule the world in peace – The Kingdom of God on Earth.

But the question is how can every single religion in the world claim the same thing, and that they are the “chosen” of God? Something is very wrong with this concept.

Other prophetic writers of the past claim that the battle of Armageddon will be spiritual in nature, rather than physical. Once the Angels of Light and His followers defeat the Angel of Darkness and his "troops", they will be thrown into the "Lake of Fire”, destroying them forever.

Strangely enough, whether or not we realize it, we are witnessing the Earth making a great transition from the third dimension into the fourth and fifth dimensions. But, no evil will be allowed in either of these dimensions, and all evil must be removed from Terra prior to this transition. Total harmony and balance must be restored to Terra.

This battle is both physical and spiritual, and has been occurring on Terra (Earth) for hundreds of thousands of years, and it is nearly over. The forces of darkness have suffered great losses, so the Draconian/Reptilian controllers have been leaving Earth. Just recently, the Forces of Light have placed a protective energy field around Earth to prevent these negative entities from returning for at least 2,000 years. Along with the physical front, hundreds of thousands of negative government leaders in positions of authority, such as administration, supervisors, attorney, bankers, judges, military commanders, doctors, teachers and clergymen have also chosen to leave Earth. There may very well be people you know who are missing.

So, who are the 'people of the lie'? They are the adherents to the religions with their followers who believe in the infallibility of their "holy" book, The Bible. All of them believe that their "gods" are good and benevolent and that they are part of the "chosen peoples". They look forward to living in a world of peace and happiness, and above all, where they would rule the world.

For centuries, religious belief systems all over the world have believed the nonsense that is recorded in the Holy Bible, without realizing that they are the perpetuators of the lie. But, in reality, they are victims.

In their Bibles, it is written that god will come and destroy all evil and the Earth, while they say that the signs are happening, and other signs are yet to be.

Exploring the Truth

Time Travel, if possible, would allow someone to visit their past at any point in history. Example: A person lives in a time that boasts events that they believe should not be, according to him, or to a group, to change the events, one or more would travel into their past. Of course, these travelers would only be looking at their own time and events, not really caring about their ancestors. In other words...it's a subjective point of view. However, these time travelers would tell someone in the past what will happen if they do not change their current events, and perhaps it is written by people in the current time. The time travelers would return to their own time in the hope that the people in the past will change their time, and thus, anything including a document, book, or other media, would also cross time into the future changing the events. So, the bad events in the future will automatically be changed as well as everything that their ancestors had accomplished in the past that was written. Then, another might think that all that is needed to change things is simply thought.

Religions are the best example of this. They use the Bible to create fear, and teach their congregations a certain way to do, think, and live. In truth, however, the religious figures we all know, need the fear to sustain their energy. They feed off our fear. In addition, people are bringing these events into being, because of *thought*. However, people do not realize that all we need to do is to change our way of thinking, while at the same time, we must remove ourselves from the Bible. There are no god(s) bringing these events into being. We only assign these people the title of "god(s)". Thought, teaching, and misunderstanding of this all lead to deep-seated fears, and the process is a never ending circle. A paradox, if you will.

We are entering a New Age. The battle we have been waging for eons is nearly over, and the "*Age of Light*" is upon us and, once it begins, Terra (Earth) and its people will never, again, see evil play any part in their life. So, this question begs and answer from you. Will you move with Terra and the Children of Light into the higher dimensions, or will you remain in this third dimensional planet to continue the status quo?

Ponder for a moment. Those who choose to remain in the third dimension will no longer be part of this World, while Earth and its enlightened people move forward into the fourth and fifth dimensions of peace, light, balance, and harmony. As this star system completes its travel around the galaxy, our group of stars will enter a new age and new cycle, and it will truly be a very interesting time for all beings within this group of stars and the Milky Way Galaxy.

The ancient Guardians of the "Universal Knowledge of the Energy Life Force" are the highest universal beings that exist in all universes, which surround humans. And, they hold the key to this knowledge, but is beyond human minds of today. These beings know that this knowledge belongs to all of us, and they also believe that it is the human right to the understanding of it. They are not to be looked upon as gods or your creators or as devils, because they were never meant to have these titles. Those titles were given to them 6-10 thousand years ago, which only served to bring fear into the people of this world. They are simply a collection of many races from across the universes.

The people of Earth, along with other beings within the Milky Way Galaxy – no matter what dimension – are about to experience the reawakening of this knowledge. Taking this quantum leap into consciousness, brings with it great discipline and training as humans learn this knowledge of the universal energy. "The human species" holds, within their consciousness, the knowledge of the universe, and we must realize our own place and responsibility. Remember that this same knowledge has been withheld from humans by all religions on Earth, and these religions have been denying you opportunity to realize, and become, who you really are as conscious beings. By removing the physical limitations of this physical plane, time is the most important resource we have. Time does not really exist, and is completely mankind's invention. It exists, only, within the physical realm of Earth. This is why when predictions do not materialize, there is frustration, and thus, believe something will never happen – limitations serve to only hinder the spiritual growth for evolution into a higher awareness of truth and wisdom. By doing so, it prevents us from evolving into the next level of knowledge and consciousness.

All religions state that during the "End Times", there will be three days of total darkness. However, those that are loyal to their gods will be removed from the Earth, and God will destroy the entire Earth from its existence.

December 21, 2012

The date, 12/21/12, is feared by religious figures around the world. But, why? Along with the fact that they refuse to tell us the truth, they have been waiting and watching for this event over the past one thousand years. For them, prophecies concerning a world destroyer will come at that time. The destroyer is called by many names: Wormwood, Marduk, and The Dark

World. It also has other names, but they have been forgotten. Recently, we have been told that our system has another planet that cannot be seen. Until now, we have only had allusions to it, and this unknown planet enters the inner star system between every 3,600 to 4,000 years, bringing with it the ability that can destroy the Earth as we know it.

Before brushing this ancient idea off, please note that as recently as 2014, surprise that a dwarf planet has been found at the outer edges of our solar system. It is a pink planet that is frozen to its core. Some also suspect, now, that another, unseen planet is somewhere out there that is larger than the Earth. This little planet is about 280 miles in diameter, and it takes at least 4,000 years to orbit our sun. Surprisingly, the time period coincides with the ancient beliefs. And, if true, then this planet may be the mysterious "Planet X", or "Nibiru", perhaps larger than Jupiter, supposedly has a "burning moon" that acts as its own sun. Some believe the earthquakes that we feel today all over the world, and the increase, may very well be caused by Nibiru's approach. It is also legend that a race lives on this planet, and they are called "The Annunaki" - beings who supposed taught man many things the last time the planet was close.

For those who are ready to lift the veils of illusions from their consciousness, the truth of the meaning of the term Armageddon / Judgment are humans' undoing – not the so-called gods / devils. All human beings must take the responsibility of our own judgment, along with the idea of the battle of light and dark. No one is going to take on this battle. Each of us must remove the veils of illusions from our consciousness, and become one with everything that surrounds mankind.

Another POV

December 21, 2012 is also based on the Mayan culture, which disappeared over 1,000 years ago. All the planets, along with our star, Apsu, aligns with the star Ophiuchus, and these two stars will align with the center of the Milky Way Galaxy.

When this does happen, the storehouse of ancient technology, the knowledge of the beginning of life within this star system, and realizing that billions of other races have been visiting planets that exist among the Milky Way Galaxy, as well as the surrounding nearby Galaxies.

We will experience a band of violet-purple light of energy as the sky begins to become even brighter with each passing year. The next evolution will transform everything into the new multi-dimensional beings as we are awakened while the next step will be a Quantum Leap into Consciousness. In addition, to those the Guardians of the knowledge of the Universes, both seen and unseen, the Ancient Beings of Beings will stand beside the Ascended ones. While the violet-purple light continues its travels, The Milky Way Galaxy will become a place of light, peace, and harmony.

The night sky will remain this way through the entire cycle of the age of Aquarius. Our immediate star group will last for 2,150 years when another new Age for Earth will begin in the year 4,150.

No one knows what 2012 will hold at this point. All we can do is look at what has been foretold about the future based on writings from those ancient civilizations. 2012 has been foretold that the Earth will be inundated by many things: mass destruction, uplifting of the soul / spirit, a great planetary alignment of our planets with several stars of our Milky Way Galaxy, the arrival of several types of ancient star beings returning back to the earth. Even more prophecies were added to the growing list. A great battle of beings of Light and Dark for control of the Earth, the rising of ancient continents from the oceans, surfacing to reveal those ancient civilizations, and put to rest our questions once and for all.

But, mankind will still be living on this earth with a better understanding about our roles in life. Perhaps not all will understand, but enough of us will.

Only time will tell us whether or not these prophecies of the past will come true. When December 21, 2012 has come and gone, will humans have a new story to tell?

Dimensional Shift

Since 1940, Earth energy has exponentially accelerated to begin the fourth dimensional shifting, and we are now in the forth the Age of Aquarius. We are leaving the third dimension behind us. Between 1989-1993, the Earth's frequencies have begun to accelerated once again after a lull, and it is seen in the weather and climate, quite literally, changing instantaneously. From that time, things have not been the same, and it will continue to change, dramatically, through 2020-2035.

After the New Millennium has passed, and between 2005-2020, people will notice a dramatic change in the planet that they can no longer pretend is not happening. Earth will be literally torn pulled apart – and, Earth will separate, and two worlds of Earth will appear. Remember in early chapters that I mentioned a time that the earth would go through a time of darkness and a time of light for three days or more. This is part of that dimensional shift, and has several names associated with it: The End Times, The Photon Belt, and The Masic Ring. "I have deemed this, The Ultrale Energy”. Terra will be torn apart as she separates into two planets – one planet will remain as it was, and which will remain in the third dimension. Those who learn at a slower pace will occupy this Earth as well as war, conflicts, and to discover their place in life. There will be no knowledge of the other world that has been created.

The second Earth will morph from the third dimension into the fourth dimension around 2100-2150. At that time, the world will become aware of their sister world that had separated from them a long time ago, and will be allowed a limited interaction, before returning back to their own world of forth dimension.

The second planet will have its Quantum Leap in Ascension by existing in the fourth and fifth dimensions simultaneously. The beings of this world will be aware of the third dimensional planet, and will be able to interact with those beings, while continuing to assist them in their Spiritual growth. A new belief system will be structured, and for this fourth and fifth dimensional world, time will no longer exist. These Beings will be free from linear time and space making them multi-dimensional beings.

Emergence process of Ascension

Some will be in awe of this; a few will be spell bound; some will not know what to think, while the rest of you will know It To Be The Truth of things. As I mentioned through the entire book, the actual records of what "I have written, will be revealed to you, and to all life on Terra in time". That moment is approaching far more quickly than mankind can imagine. Some will not be prepared, while others are waiting for this time to arrive.

This knowledge has been awakened slowly for the past 5,000 years during the time when our Earth entered the age of Aries, and finally to enter the age of Pisces, which were the time of conflicts, wars, and confusion. In the year 1800, we entered the Age of Aquarius, the age of peace, light, and emergence. We will be traveling this age for at least 200, or more, and will continue to evolve humanity to the point of the Dimensional Shift, and to bring humanity to this point, and will arrive between 2010-2025, when the full consciousness of humanity will transition to Ascension – a Quantum Leap into a full, Spiritual Re-Awakening!

The knowledge was assembled for one reason, and one only – that all life in existence should be taught the Universal Laws. These Laws consist of information about the steps of evolution on all planes of existence. The Guardians of the Universal Laws would impart these laws to life on all planets planes, and dimensions to help the inhabitants understand their importance in life. There are times that several Guardians will manifest upon a plane if the inhabitants need that type of effect to bring the Universal Knowledge to them.

In the Bible, as well as other documents around the world, several beings lived to be around 6-9 hundred years of age. About 8,000 years ago, there was a time when all beings lived several hundreds of years. These Beings came here from all corners of the Universes to help all Star Civilizations, and to awake the Knowledge of Ascension that is within every being. And, it still exists today, within one's own mind. It is also available in tangible documents located in various places in the world.

One of these is within the archive of the Vatican. We have only been allowed the distorted versions of this knowledge, while the real knowledge has been hidden where only a few have access to it. It is forbidden to all but those few. You have been told through the religions, through the Ages, that no one can have Eternal Life (Ascension), and only the gods has the right to Eternal Life, or when you drink from the cup of Christ. The truth is that the decision to Ascend is with every being. You must believe in yourself and knowing that it is the Master plan of Eternal Life, each human can choose how long the Eternal Life will be for them.

Of course, you chose how long that Eternal Life would be. Ascension comes from using the Universal energies and Love, when used in unison with other key factors. You need to work with those energies and you need to know how to bring the energies into your being. Your physical, spiritual teachers, along with Spiritual guides, will show you the true way to Ascension. Avoid any being claiming to be god, or the devil, because they cover your eyes with veils of illusions. While they will not claim that they are your gods, they will claim that they are gods unto themselves.

A final thought....We Are One With Everything!

We were once where you are now,
When the truth is known!
You will be where we are now,
When you understand the universe!

We were once like you,
Before our evolution!
You will become as we are now,
When you accept the "Universal Knowledge of Truth".

All being will begin the evolutional ladder with this knowledge. But, it is the moment of truth for humans that has finally arrived to claim your rite of passage to this knowledge; to know who you are as beings of consciousness; to take your place amongst the countless other beings that came before mankind; to take the quantum leap into consciousness, which is rightfully ours. End the control of these beings in human existence. Becoming awakened will allow man to learn of the truth, and then humans will no longer be able to be controlled. Once man is no longer controlled, then wars and division on Earth will also be at an end. At that time, the next cycle within the New Age can finally begin. Take responsibility for your own thoughts and the creations that come from those thoughts. In light of this, please take a moment to reflect on the following questions:

- Is this the way man should continue living complete with wars and fear, which all governments have sanctioned over the course of the last 25,000 years, or should humans live in peace and harmony with all beings as well as each other?
- Is this the way man should continue living bowing to religious belief systems that tell you what to think and do?

Remember, all governments and religions do not want peace and harmony, for without this power of fear over mankind, they can no longer control mankind. So, it is up to man to decide if they want the "New Cycle, New Age" to enter our lives so that we may have a world of peace, harmony to join with other groups of beings within our Milky Way Galaxy?

There is no reason to wait. It's time for the decision to made. Tell the Universe that you no longer want to be controlled by fear, and you demand that the fear and wars end immediately! This brings you to your next step on the evolution ladder and it takes you to, The Quantum Leap Into Consciousness.

I hope through my series of books that you

have a better idea of what your life is about, along with removing the veils of Illusions. If you have begun to understand all that has been written, then I have done my duty. As conscious beings, this is just the beginning! Remember, it is the responsibility of those who have awakened to teach those who have yet to do so.

Remember this...the Knowledge of Life is available for all to learn, and not for just a select few. No one being has the exclusive rights to the true knowledge of life. It is for all.

This is not the beginning of the end…
It is also not the end…
It is of a new beginning…
It is leaving of the old ways behind
to begin our lives anew...

As you might remember within Book 1 of "A Journey Into The Spiritual Quest Of Who We Are – The Reawakening", I mentioned that there would be a quantum leap of Terra around the year, 2020. One earth will stay in the 3rd dimension for those that need more time to make the transition to their full potential, but continuing to live in denial and continuing on with warfare. While the people of the 2nd world become the conscious beings who have already reached theirs unfolding it in my first book, "A Journey Into The Spiritual Quest Of Who We Are - Book 1 The

Reawakening" in 1987. Time will cease to exist from this point forward.

Since 1990, some have already changed their thoughts realizing that they created the world around them. And, some older generations of negative thoughts regarding fear, war, and destruction have left this planet behind, while a new generation is being born. These people believe that it is time for peace and a union between all beings that are in existence. After this transition is completed, and we enter into the New Age, it will feel as if the planet has become larger. But in fact, the population will be dramatically reduced to those who wish to evolve spiritually and peacefully.

Can mankind really learn from the past? Are we doomed to continue the opposite? At this point in time, the answer is probably no. The battle between good and evil to possess Earth continues. Governments and religions continue to control, still causing fear.

1985 ended the current age known as the Piscean Age lasting about 6 thousand years – a dark age for all – causing war, turmoil, fear, conflicts, and controlling the masses through deceptions by creating "gods" and "demons" simply by saying it was true by creating negative thoughts. And, we believed it.

From 1985 – 2020 was known as the transition period during the age of Pisces. But, our star system the need for this negative energy no longer exits. Earth no longer has need for it, especially as the world journeys into the next age. It is time to restructure views and thoughts, and to leave the negative part of our lives go for they are no longer a part of, the New Age of Aquarius – The Age of Light. And, this restructure will last between 2000-2012, and then, begins the New Age known as the Aquarian Age of Light. No longer with the truth be suppressed. So as the earth and her people are moving forward in the evolution, so does the galaxy that we resids as well as the universe. It is the realization of who we truly are that will change everything for us. While other beings have been down this road of changing of the Ages, we also had the ability, but with the knowledge forbidden to us, all but a few remember.

Life and all Ages have one thing which is common to one another - from life to death, from death to life again – these are the cycles of the essence of Life and of the Ages – an Age of Light followed by an Age of Dark. These cycles continue over and over without end. But, even though each age goes from Light to Dark, and back again, the energy in each cycle is never the same. And, not everyone will survive these changes. The ones that do survive, will secure a very new place, a New Planet for the future, and the revelation of the Universal Knowledge.

Through this wisdom will come the everlasting peace that the Earth, along with its people on it. Besides having peace, there will also be eternal life for those who choose to exercise their free will. It will truly be a step up on the Spiritual evolutionary ladder with this unlimited Knowledge of the Universal Wisdom. Leaving the 3rd dimensional existence, man will learn to develop into multi-dimensional beings, and eventually, into the 4th and 5th dimensional existence. This is known as the Soul and Spirit, which will be able to exist outside of one another, and simultaneously coexisting with others. This is the missing link sought by man for thousands upon thousands of years.

Which this means going into the unknown, not knowing what might be coming your way, if it is for the worst or for the better for your soul? Nevertheless, either way, if you look at it now, you will benefit from your own experiences of these events that are in front of you. Of course, everything you experience will be a step up on the evolutionary scale of existence going towards becoming a multidimensional being.

Then the New Age is really, a point in time where the soul of every being has the chance to start the beginning of their new life, if it is in another cycle of life, or another dimension of existence. This is transpiring at this time for all to experience.

You are all going to be part of the changes, of course, not everyone will survive these changes. For the ones that do survive, it will be a new place, a New Planet for the future. In this cycle, there will come the revealing of the Universal Knowledge that has been kept hidden from many of you for about four thousand years. It is simply man's own free will. There are three names by which this is known.

1. The first name is called, the New Age: The beginning of transformation.
2. Second Coming of Christ: This is the awakening of the hidden knowledge that Emmanuel (Jesus) once taught. The coming of the second Christ is not a single person that has the same powers that Jesus once had. It is all who have chosen.
3. The God Source: Which is the involvement in the Universal Mind, all souls acting as one, the ultimate creator. All being will possess it.

I is now time to choose. It will be here much faster than expected. Are people ready to choose the Light instead of the dark? Are will choose the same path as many has always chosen? It's up to each individual to choose by using their free will.

References

The zoroastrian 15 book series from 4,000 bce-1,000 bce, translation by joseph h. Peterson 1997

Grecian history, 1892 by james richard joy

The bundahishn (creation) or knowledge from the zand, 1897 by e.w. west

Counsels of adarbad mahraspandan (the teachings of the magi) 1956 by r.c. zaehner

The knigdom of lu, 1929 by maurice magre

Aphrodite, 1932 by pierre louys

Oahspe a new bible, fifth american edition 1942 by anno kosmon

The age of fable, or the beuties of mythology, 1942 by thomas bulfinch

The world's religions revise, 1954 by charles s. Braden

The wisdom of the living religions, 1956 seventh printing by joseph gear

Hinduism, great religions of modern man, second printing 1961 by george braziller

Living religions of the world, 1962 by fredreric spiegelberg

The comparative study of religions, fifth printing 1969 by joachim wach

Holly bible, (rsv, revised standard version) 1972 edtion by thomas nelson

Holly bible, (kjv, king james version) 1985 edtion, by the gideons international

The book of mormon, 1963 the church of jesus christ of latter-day saints, by david o. Mchay

The urantia book, sixth printing 1978
by urantia foundation

The twelfth planet, the earth chronicles, 1978 by zecharia sitchin

Christian churches of god, 1997 australia
the elect as elohim
the meaning of the names of gods
light bearer and the morning star
abracadabra the meaning of names

Frobidden knowledge, 1996 by roger shattuck

Hinduism, the journey of self discovery, 1997 by a.c. bhaktivedanta swami prabhupada

Hinduism, the science of self realization 1997 by a.c. bhaktivedanta swami prabhupada

Hinduism, bhagavad-gita as it is, sixth printing 1994 by a.c. bhaktivedante swami prabhupada

The templar revelation, secret guardians of the true identity of christ, 1998 by lynn pickett, clive prince

Some film related:

All films on the bible stories of creation

Lord of the ring series by jrr tolken

Star wars 1977-2005 by george lucus

Stargate movies/tv series

Contact 1997 movie with jodie foster

Also other materials such as:
atlantis, lemuria, mu

Mythology series, by joseph campbell 1983

Highlander Movies and TV Series

Pictures throughout this Book, are from assortment of bibles and online

www.ingramcontent.com/pod-product-compliance
Lightning Source LLC
Chambersburg PA
CBHW070027120726
47909CB00003B/1082

* 9 7 8 0 9 7 6 7 8 3 2 9 9 *